The Missing Flower Child

A Vivian Kessler Case

B.A. Montes

Contents

1

PART I—NOVEMBER RAIN

"Every soul comes with a shadow. Some just learn to dance with theirs better than others."—Seamus

***

2

SAFE HAVEN

THURSDAY, NOVEMBER 13, 1975

"It's seven o'clock, straight up in the Windy City. This is WGN Radio, 720 on your dial. Our top story tonight: Alabama Governor George Wallace declares he's in for the '76 presidential race. Here in Chicago, police report a body of an unidentified young woman found near the lakefront this afternoon. No further details released. In sports, the Blackhawks face Detroit at the Stadium. Puck drops at 7:30. The forecast calls for a chilly night—flurries likely by morning. Updates next hour. You're listening to WGN radio."

It was Thursday, November 13, 1975—just another night in Chicago, another client to meet: a Vietnam veteran.

The music drifted from her radio—*Like a Rhinestone Cowboy*—thin and tinny, like a jukebox two rooms over. Vivian never touched the dial. WGN was the only station worth hearing—at least that's what Mags O'Connell, her longtime mentor, used to say.

The refrigerator's hum and the wind slipping through a cracked window competed for space. The screech of the El overhead. No one listened anymore.

A half-finished mug of coffee, an ashtray crowded with cigarettes burned halfway down, and her notebook sat on the Formica table.

Out there, noise and neon staple shut. In here, it's the calm between storms. Apartment 2, Lake Street.

An old two-flat, nothing fancy, but it was hers. Vivian Kessler, PI.

She underlined her last note, laid down her pen, and snapped the book shut. Secrets didn't stay locked, but they stayed put in her notebook.

Seamus's words came back to her. She wasn't sure if it was wisdom or just the talk you heard over too many drinks, but tonight it fit.

For an instant she flashed back to another November, another kind of shine—herself as a girl, tucked against her mother on the Ravenswood El, shoulder to wool, the smell of winter in the train car. She remembered the crowd spilling onto State Street—frosted glass, toy trains, mannequins in tinsel. Marshall Field's windows had shimmered like promises. That was once. Now the only windows she watched rattled in their frames, catching the red strobe of an ambulance before it tore past. Chicago hadn't stopped glowing. It just lit different things.

As she rose, she stubbed out the last of her cigarette, and her boots scuffed the linoleum—ready to roll. She slipped into her brown overcoat. Gloves next—left first, tugged tight at the wrist.

Her purse slumped against the chair, worn smooth by years of use. She dropped the notebook inside, pen tucked alongside. She swung it over her shoulder. The purse fell into place at her hip, a weight that steadied more than it burdened. Her final ritual.

The alley window caught her reflection in the glass—ghosted, the past still there.

Vivian glanced at the clock. "*Time's up,*" she muttered. "*Gotta go.*"

She pulled her coat tighter, her boots striking a steady rhythm on the worn floorboards. The room carried its ghosts quietly—the Leica camera catching the light, a folded flag, a letter box tied in fading ribbon. She lingered there, fingers brushing the edge of the shelf. *Another soldier—another story,* she thought. *Too many that ended before they began.*

She drew a slow breath, then turned toward the window, where the city waited—gray, patient, and unchanging.

She stepped out, leaving the radio behind—a voice she never turned off, only walked away from.

***

3

The Rail

Thursday, November 13, 1975

The hallway was dark. She descended, steady, each stair groaning—giving her away like a warning bell.

Need to tell Hal to change that bulb.

A door handle turned below.

"Is that you, Viv?" called Hal Russo.

"Hello, Hal. Hallway light's out," Vivian replied.

"I'll get to it in the morning. You heading out?"

"Keep the place safe while I'm gone," she told him.

Hal pointed his Pabst can at her, spilling foam onto his Bears sweatshirt.

"I will. Be careful out there, Viv."

She passed the two chipped mailboxes, footsteps tapping across the cracked mosaic tile. As she opened the door, the wind bit the bare skin of her face. She started her walk, one focus—the warm glow of the bar, down the block, under the tracks.

A dead neon tube sagged from the old Lakeview Drugs sign; its Rexall glow long gone. The boarded windows were a patchwork of plywood and old graffiti. A bus shuddered past, exhaust spreading a bitter scent, drowning the last trace of coffee from the Lake Street Grill.

She kept moving. She caught the alley's shadow in passing—a darkness she chose not to linger on. Her mind was already at the Rail, bracing for whatever her client would leave unsaid.

People never told the whole truth—only the parts they could live with. The mess came later.

As she neared the corner, two women stepped out of Art's Tap—the first in a black coat, cigarette glowing like a tiny warning light; the other a redhead laughing softly, her breath a cloud in the cold. They lingered under the awning, then turned separate ways without a word.

The Old-Style decal in the window at Art's Tap next door to The Brass Rail curled in the dim light, Schlitz and Pabst fading from her younger nights. Chicago always backed the home team, even in bitter winters. *Eddie ought to swap that Schlitz sign,* she thought. *Show he's still on the town's side.*

The door held firm against the stiff November wind. She pushed through.

The jukebox snapped to life—the Chi-Lites' *Have You Seen Her* poured through the speakers, a velvet voice, strings curling into the quiet.

Eddie, in a bright white shirt and too-tight suspenders, looked up from behind the bar, glass and rag in hand.

At the far end, Seamus shifted on his stool, his gray beard softening the lines of age. The whiskey had a way of settling into him, same as the years did—slow, steady, without apology. Beside him sat Frank, solid as a post, a man built on silence and habit. The kind who still carried the posture of the badge he'd left behind in New York. His glass caught the dim light, its scent sharp, familiar, comforting.

Vivian stepped inside, the song washing over her.

Eddie's hand faltered—the glass slipped, a splash of water catching the light. He steadied it, eyes fixed a beat too long on the jukebox as a soulful voice asked after someone who never came home.

***

4

LETTERS

THURSDAY, NOVEMBER 13, 1975

Eddie tuned the radio, settling in for the hockey broadcast. "Same as always, Viv?"

"Just water."

"A Michigan Straight, then," he teased.

"Tap's fine," she said.

Usually good company, Frank and Seamus were lost in their own thoughts. The bar was still, no surprise for a Thursday night. She glanced at the clock—7:35. The client must be running late.

Eddie set a glass of water on the bar. Then the door opened. A figure stepped in, shrouded in shadows. Vivian knew the look—rigid shoulders, scanning eyes, a body that trailed behind. The soldier's posture tugged at something she thought she'd buried long ago.

Behind the bar, Eddie fumbled the glass, catching it just before it slipped. His eyes darted to the doorway, then skittered away too fast. He forced the rag back into motion, shoulders hunched as though hoping no one had noticed.

Something in the room shifted. A low hum, the buzz of neon, cut through the quiet. From the street, the draft carried grit from the street. The weight in the air told her this case would tangle.

Vivian turned back to the bar, set her boot on the bar rail, and waited. If he were Peter Mitchell, he'd come to her. He stopped at her side. For a moment, nothing. Just the neon hum and the faint clink of glass. Then, awkwardly—"Vivian Kessler?"

She didn't turn. "Who's asking?"

Behind her, Eddie slid down the bar, ready to serve.

"Peter Mitchell," he said, the name almost catching in his throat. He shifted his weight, eyes flicking to the glass in front of her before settling back on her face.

"Detective Callahan. Nineteenth District. He... he said you were the one to talk to."

Vivian finally turned, one hand still on her glass. "Tommy Callahan sent you my way?"

He nodded. "Callahan said you've got a thing for the cases nobody downtown wants."

Her lips curved, not quite a smile. "That sounds like Tommy." Vivian shrugged off her jacket; the faint rustle broke the quiet. "Eddie, get the kid a drink."

She lifted her gloves, tapped them once against the wood, then nodded toward the booth by the jukebox—her office.

"Let's talk."

Peter glanced at Eddie. "Beer, please." His voice steadied a little with the word. Eddie nodded, pulling a tap. Only then did Peter follow as Vivian slid into the booth.

The jukebox clicked and spun—Bill Withers, *Ain't No Sunshine.* Shadows deepened with every note. She leaned back, set her gloves on the table, and let the silence stretch. Finally, she fixed him with a look. "What do you want, Peter?"

Eddie arrived with the beer, set it down without a word. Foam slid down the glass.

Peter wrapped his hand around the glass but didn't drink. His eyes stayed fixed on the beer, jaw tight. "It's my sister," he said finally. "Donna."

Vivian waited, still as smoke.

"She wrote all through my second tour—said San Francisco felt alive, like people finally meant all that talk about peace and love. After I got back, the letters kept coming for a while. Then one letter showed up this summer, postmarked Chicago—said she might come home for good. After that... nothing."

He drew a slow breath, eyes on the glass in front of him. "When the letters stopped, I figured she'd already made it back. I went to the cops here in August, tried to file a report. Missing adults—they don't rush on those. Weeks went by, and every call felt colder. Only one detective—Callahan—took me seriously. Said if anyone could find her, it'd be you."

Vivian leaned in; eyes steady. "That all you've got?"

Peter hesitated, then reached into his jacket. He slid two things across the table: a worn photograph of Donna on the streets of Haight-Ashbury—beads and flowers tangled in her hair—and a folded letter, creased soft from too many readings.

"It's all I've got," he whispered. "Her last one from California. The one she sent before she talked about coming home. I gave the Chicago letter to the cops—they never gave it back."

Vivian studied them in silence, her expression unreadable.

"Anything else?"

He frowned, searching the table as if the answer might hide there. "Not really. There was this girl she mentioned once—Micky, maybe? Or Nikki? Said she'd met her at some shop or party. Probably nothing." He gave a half-shrug. "Donna wrote about everyone as if they were soul mates."

Vivian didn't press. She simply nodded, filing both names away. "Anything else?"

Peter's eyes narrowed, as though chasing something half-remembered. Then he gave a small nod, almost relieved. "Yeah—she's got a little tattoo behind her ear. A blue star. Said it'd keep her from getting lost. My mother hated it."

Vivian paused, photo still between her fingers. She studied it again—the angle of the girl's face; the hair covering just enough. No mark. Her voice came quiet. "Let's hope it did."

She glanced once more at the photo and letter, then slipped them into her purse.

Peter looked up again. "How much? I—I don't have a lot of money."

Vivian studied him—the stiffness in his shoulders, the eyes that scanned without rest. She'd seen that before. Different man, different war, same weight carried home.

She set her gloves flat on the table, voice even. "Don't worry about the money, Peter. We'll work it out."

For the first time all night, her tone softened—just a fraction. She let the silence stretch before leaning in. "When was the last time anyone here saw her?"

Peter frowned, searching the table again. "I thought she was back, but nobody's seen her lately. I don't even know for sure when she left California."

Vivian tapped a finger against the table, steady and patient. "Does she have friends here? A place she stayed?"

He shook his head, then hesitated. "There were names once—people she ran with. Can't remember most of them now." He exhaled through his nose. "Folks said she was hard to find. Different after San Francisco. My parents said that too."

Vivian nodded once, filing it all away. "All right. How do I reach you?"

"I'm staying at the Y on LaSalle," he said. "Room 12. They'll get me a message."

Vivian gave a nod. "Thanks, Peter."

She rose, slipping into her jacket, purse over her shoulder. Peter stayed put, finally lifting his beer, the foam gone flat. A kid fresh out of the jungle, chasing a ghost. She'd seen it before—men trying to fight what followed them home. And now he'd done the only thing he could: handed her the pieces.

Before turning to the door, Vivian glanced toward the far end of the bar. Frank looked up first, the look that asked if she was all right without saying it. She gave him a nod—answer enough between old colleagues. Seamus sat beside him, turning his glass absently, eyes half on the jukebox, half somewhere past it. A man who'd seen too much but kept it to himself. Vivian offered them a thin smile. "Quiet night, boys. I've got to go."

The jukebox flipped, and the soulful sound of Gladys Knight and the Pips filled the air, singing of a *Midnight Train to Georgia.*

Vivian tipped her chin at Eddie. "Try not to polish the bar down to the grain before I get back."

She moved toward the door, her heels keeping time with the music.

Behind her, Seamus leaned closer to Frank, voice low but certain.

"Storm's coming."

Thursday night air hit cold as a promise.

***

5

The Ankh

Thursday, November 13, 1975

The El thundered above as she stepped into the night, the street trembling beneath her boots. From the open door came one fading echo—a woman's voice promising she'd follow love wherever it led.

Vivian paused at the curb, watching the sparks die out along the track. *Everyone lived in someone's world*, she thought. *The trick was remembering which one was yours.*

The walk back home was short: a block of cracked pavement and shuttered storefronts. She passed the dark alley again, shadows thick as tar between the brick walls. It breathed cold against her as she went by—the alley that made everyone remember something they'd rather forget.

At the corner stood her building, worn brick, a sagging stoop. She stepped into the entryway—no Hal this time. The air carried the faint smell of old wood and boiled cabbage, same as always. She climbed the stairs in silence.

Inside, she peeled off the day—blouse first, then skirt—and slipped into an oversized men's white shirt. The sleeves hung loosely as she rolled them past her wrists. The boots stayed on.

She carried her purse to the kitchen table and sat. From the purse came the photograph and the folded letter. Beside them she laid her notebook and pen—a slim black Parker with tiny M.O. initials etched near the clip. She never wrote without it.

First came the photo, a perfectly still image meant to be remembered forever. In Haight-Ashbury, Donna's youthful expression was striking—her flowing hair framing a neck adorned with bead chains and a wide, open smile. Vivian studied the picture, her fingers brushing the rough edges. Then she saw the T-shaped pendant—a small brass ankh, handmade and dulled with age, its surface catching just a trace of light, a symbol of life.

With a narrowed gaze fixed on the necklace, Vivian quickly jotted a note in the margin of her pad. She set down the pen and reached for the letter.

For a moment, her own past tugged at her—letters still tucked in a box in her closet, folded soft from rereading, written by two men who never came home. Words of youth and hope, just like Donna's, chasing dreams that didn't survive the war.

Donna's handwriting was looping and free, though the ink was a little smudged.

Dear Peter,

I keep thinking back to Woodstock. That's where it all started for me—the music, the feeling that we could change the world.

For a while, I believed it. I thought if I just kept following that road, I'd find the truth everyone was singing about.

That's what brought me to San Francisco. At first, it really felt like freedom—the parks full of music, colors in the streets, people talking about peace like it was something you could touch. I still want to believe it's out here somewhere, but it's harder now. The drugs don't fix the loneliness, and the boys with guitars aren't the men they pretend to be.

Sometimes I miss home—Dad's gruff voice at dinner. And Mom, humming along with the radio while she cooked, pretending not to listen when we argued. I don't tell anyone that. You're supposed to be free, not homesick. But I am. More than a little, maybe. I've been thinking about coming back. Chicago might not be paradise, but at least it's ours.

I met a girl who knows a guy back in the city—he runs a little shop on Milwaukee Avenue, selling jewelry and old records. She says he gets things from all over, even Haight Street. Maybe I'll stop in when I'm home, see if it feels as strange as she made it sound.

Mostly, I just miss you. Can't wait for your tour to be over—to see you, to laugh the way we used to. Knowing you'll be back soon makes it easier to hold on out here.

I'll be fine; don't worry. If I come back to Chicago, I'll figure things out. I want to be somebody, Peter. Haven't quite found out who yet. But I will. Knowing you're out there keeps me strong.

Love always, Donna

Vivian let the page rest, the words pulling at her—youth and hope inked on paper, but beneath them a tremor, a drift. She reached for her pen again, underlining two phrases in the margin: coming back and Milwaukee Avenue. The first spoke of longing; the second of direction. Together, they felt like a trail.

Her eyes returned to the photograph, narrowing on the necklace—a tiny clue Donna hadn't known she'd given. The picture and the note pointed to the same place.

Vivian turned the ankh in her mind, the imagined smoothness sparking a flash of memory—a case years back when a near-twin of the charm had gleamed in a pawnshop window on Milwaukee Avenue. That job ended in betrayal and a body cooling on a cold, unforgiving slab. The echo of that case clung to her like the November chill. Some streets never let go. Milwaukee Avenue was calling again.

She closed the notebook and leaned back in her chair. Outside, the El's hum faded beneath the wind's long sigh. The city never really slept—but she'd try.

She turned out the light, but the dark shifted—like film catching between frames. The sound of distant thunder might've been a train, or something older she'd never outrun. Somewhere behind her eyelids, jungle heat gathered, and the night began to remember for her.

Tomorrow, Milwaukee Avenue.

***

6

PART II—THE DARK CITY

***

7

— · —

MICK

Friday, November 14, 1975

Gunfire first—distant, muffled, like firecrackers underwater.

The jungle pressed in, damp air clinging to her skin. Mick's voice crackled through static, urgent, nearly gone before she caught it. The mud pulled at her boots. Flashes lit the trees—muzzle or lightning, it didn't matter. Smoke thickened. Mick blurred into shadow, camera swinging, then dropped into the dirt.

Her arms felt heavy as stone as she reached for him. Cordite and rain filled her lungs. Then came the shriek—metal tearing through jungle, until it was only her heartbeat.

Vivian snapped awake to the alarm's buzz at 6:45. Friday, November 14, 1975.

The city outside hadn't thawed since yesterday.

Mick stared back from the photo on her nightstand, eyes as exact as his lens had been.

Her bare feet hit the cold linoleum. Coffee on the stove, Zenith tuned to WGN—Wally Phillips sounded too cheerful for a city still half-asleep. His voice rolled past her, lost to the photograph and letter on the table.

She poured the first cup, steam rising like a small mercy, and crossed into the living room.

Petula Clark spun on the phonograph—*I Know a Place*, her old favorite, filling the room like company. She settled into the wide chair, coffee steaming beside her, and waited until the last track faded. Time to move.

Brown leather pants creaked as she dressed, coat belted, boots scuffed but sure. She stepped into the cold.

Hal was on a ladder in the hall, twisting in a new bulb.

Vivian smiled. "You're a doll, Hal."

He grinned down, boyish even in middle age. "Anything for you, Miss Viv."

The morning light caught her face as she stepped into the brittle November air. The ankh, Milwaukee Avenue, today's clues—the city waited.

***

8

— · —

MILWAUKEE

FRIDAY, NOVEMBER 14, 1975

The number 9 Ashland bus screeched to a halt. And the doors folded open with a hiss. Vivian dropped her token with a clink and slid into a window seat.

Gray streaks of the city blurred past—shuttered laundromats, bakeries steaming with kolacky and sweet rolls, factory smoke drifting low across the rooftops.

She stepped down at Division. Cabbage, pierogi, diesel, fried dough, coal dust—the Polish Triangle always hit the same way, like—memory.

The pawnshop sagged at 1147 Milwaukee, just as she remembered. Faded brick, windows jammed with dented horns and busted watches, junk that had outlived its owners. The door gave with a push, and the bell let out a tired, dusty ring.

From the back came Lenny Kowalski, wiping his hands on a rag, sweat shining under the weak light. His face soured at the sight of her.

"Well, well. Vivian Kessler."

She held out Donna's photo, finger tapping the ankh at her throat. "Seen one of these lately?"

He squinted. "Necklaces like that? Common. A dime a dozen."

"Not this one."

The rag stopped moving. Silence thickened. He wasn't cracking—he was calculating. She'd seen that flicker before, back when he'd danced around the Ashland case.

He turned away, rummaging through a drawer of pawn tags. With his back turned, Vivian observed the counter, which displayed rings, lighters, a cracked cigarette case, and a pile of pawn slips under a chipped glass tray. One page half-hung over the edge, the corner darkened with grease pencil:

".38 revolver—no serial—sold cash; 10/28"

She slid it free with one finger, folded it into her glove. The movement was slight, invisible, the kind that belonged to someone who'd learned long ago when to steal and when to watch.

Kowalski straightened, voice too smooth. "Maybe check the clubs around here. Trinkets like that pass through plenty of hands."

Vivian met his eyes, the smile she gave him measured and thin. 'I'll do that.'

The bell scraped thin as she stepped into the cold.

Outside, she leaned against the brick, breath fogging in the wind, and unfolded the slip. The date—October 28. Was that the week Donna vanished?

A gun, cash, no serial number. And a buyer who didn't sign his name.

She slipped it back into her glove and started walking.

Callahan was next.

***

9

CALLAHAN

FRIDAY, NOVEMBER 14, 1975

The northbound No. 9 lurched and groaned, hauling her past storefront churches and brick flats where laundry sagged from lines like tired flags. The ride rocked steady, her thoughts drifting—Mick's last dispatch from Saigon, her father pointing out the Town Hall station, her mother's sauerbraten simmering on a back burner. Chicago carried its ghosts lightly, but they never let go.

The Town Hall precinct sat just off Halsted and Addison, the old Lake View station still holding its corner after all these years. The brick worn pale, limestone streaked with soot. Inside, the air stank of cigarettes and burned coffee. Phones rang, typewriters clattered, radios hissed, same chaos, just slower hands running it.

Vivian moved through the bullpen.

Nameplates hadn't changed; only the eyes behind them—tired, half-bought.

At the far end, Callahan leaned back in his chair, laughter low into the phone. Then he saw her. The grin that spread across his face was the kind that had smoothed over lies and opened doors—sometimes the same ones.

He hung up. "Kessler. Hell of a way to brighten my afternoon."

"Not if you're paying attention," she said, resting a hand on his chair. "Remember that soldier you sent me—the one looking for his sister?"

Callahan rocked back; the chair groaned. "Yeah. Said we missed something. Looked like a runaway to me."

Vivian slid Donna's photo across the blotter. "Runaways don't leave brothers hollowed out."

He studied the picture, then the ankh, and said nothing.

"Kowalski's no help," snapped Vivian.

He snorted. "Kowalski hasn't done an honest day's work since '68." His grin lingered softly around the edges. "You always chased the hard ones, Viv."

She gave him a look sharp enough to cut paper. "Someone's got to keep you honest."

"Good luck with that." He leaned forward, voice dropping. "We had a body once—young, beads, overdose maybe. Never felt right. File disappeared when the brass wanted the streets clean."

For a second, guilt flashed behind his eyes before habit buried it. Same old Tommy—too smart to be dirty, too scared to stay clean.

"Kowalski's still moving pieces he shouldn't," she said, sliding a folded slip across the desk.

Callahan didn't touch it. Just stared at the glove she'd taken it from.

"Where'd you get this?"

"Same place you get your coffee—dirty counter, no cream."

He let out a breath through his teeth. "You keep digging like this, Viv, you're gonna end up under one of his counters."

He nodded toward her purse. "You want to see the file? Come by after hours. Nobody'll notice."

Her smile flickered. "After hours, Tommy? I'm flattered. But this isn't a date."

"Didn't say it was," he said, almost convincing himself.

She slipped the photo away. "You just did."

She dropped a dime into the pay phone down the hall. "Peter—it's Vivian. Meet me at the Lake Street Grill, five o'clock."

Half an hour later, steam fogged the glass at the Lake Street Grill. Inside, Peter hunched in a corner booth, coffee clutched too tight, grilled cheese cooling untouched.

From a counter radio, Roberta Flack's *Killing Me Softly* drifted through the hiss of the grill—too tender for the room, every note bending toward heartbreak.

She paused in the doorway, taking him in—the slumped shoulders, the untouched sandwich, the eyes that had already seen too much. Callahan's lead had turned the case; Peter just hadn't realized it yet.

Vivian slid across from him and let the silence breathe.

"Yesterday you gave me the broad strokes—Donna's letter, her friends in Haight," she said. "Callahan mentioned an unidentified body. Anything you didn't tell me?"

His jaw locked. "I told you everything."

She tilted her head, her voice dry as old paper. "You're young, Peter. You still think everything fits in one breath."

He hesitated. "There was... someone. Nikki. Not a girlfriend. Just a shadow. Always near Donna's crowd. Nobody knew where she stayed."

Vivian repeated it, low. "Nikki." The El screamed past, shaking the plates. A name with teeth.

She stood, offering him a faint smile. "Get some rest, Peter. I'll be in touch."

Outside, dusk spread thin and gold. Friday night quickened its pulse. The Brass Rail was waiting.

***

10

Ronnie

Friday, November 14, 1975

The Rail's solid door gave way to warmth, neon, and smoke. Friday night was already humming—barstools filled, glasses clinked, the jukebox pouring out Tyrone Davis crooning *Turn Back the Hands of Time*.

Eddie hurried behind the bar, sleeves damp, tray clattering in his hand. "Evenin', Viv. Usual?"

She winked. "You read me."

Seamus raised his whiskey from his stool by the jukebox. Frank, steady as stone, gave her a smile that lingered longer than it should.

"Thought you'd sworn off the hard stuff till the next storm," Seamus said, his brogue softening the tease.

Vivian slid onto her stool. "This is the next storm."

Frank chuckled, rough and low. "You never could sit one out."

"Neither could you," she said.

"Yeah," he replied, eyes on his glass. "Difference is, you still win some of yours."

Seamus tipped his glass toward her. "And she remembers the losses better than the wins. That's what keeps her sharp."

Vivian smiled faintly. "You just like reminding me I'm getting predictable."

"Predictable's safe," Seamus said. "Safe's still breathing."

The jukebox clicked to the next verse; laughter rolled from a table near the back. The bar had its own rhythm—one Vivian had learned to trust more than most people.

Then, the room shifted.

Loretta, local street seer, came in first—swagger wrapped in burgundy leather, satin flashing under neon. Her brown skin caught the amber light as she slid onto the stool, a halo of tight curls framing eyes that missed nothing. A cream vinyl mini skirt flashed as she moved, tall ivory boots snapping with each step. "Friday crowd's alive," she said, ordering with a flick of her wrist.

The door swung again, perfume and cold air riding in together. Veronica "Ronnie" Hayes followed—socialite on the make, charm sharpened to a weapon. Burnt-orange coat, yellow-and-orange dress glowing in the Rail's dim light. Tan patent-leather boots clicked deliberately, claiming ground before she spoke. She met Vivian's eyes in the mirror first—just a flicker, but enough to start the game.

"Eddie, darling," Ronnie purred, fingertip tracing the bar's edge. "Don't let a girl go thirsty."

Eddie fumbled for a clean glass, ears turning red. Loretta smirked, exhaling smoke.

"Careful, Eddie," she said. "She'll melt you down if you're not steady."

Vivian took her drink and leaned an elbow on the bar. The noise swelled, laughter, glass, the low whirl of the jukebox. She angled toward Frank, voice dropping.

"You ever hear the name Nikki—Division Street, maybe?"

"Can't say I have. You chasing ghosts again?" he said.

"Maybe one that's still breathing," she said, then let the line hang loud enough for Ronnie to hear.

Ronnie's reflection in the mirror paused mid-drag. Vivian caught it, then smiled faintly—an invitation wrapped in insult.

"You always had the best ears in the room, Ronnie," she said lightly. "I figured if there's trouble worth knowing, it probably whispered it to you first."

Ronnie turned, grin bright but eyes sharp. "Flattery? From you?"

Vivian shrugged. "Just professional curiosity. Girl named Nikki. Ring any bells?"

Ronnie took her time answering, gaze flicking to Eddie as if weighing how much to give. Vivian didn't rush; she let the silence do its work.

Finally, Ronnie laughed—low, deliberate. "Goes by Nikki," she said at last. "Pretty little thing, long hair, too much hope in her eyes. Shows up at the Vortex—talks big, but she's green. Thinks the world's still safe after midnight."

Vivian's smile cooled to glass. "Then she's in the wrong city."

Ronnie tapped ash into her drink. "Aren't we all?"

Loretta blew a thin stream of smoke, voice dry. "Rail hears plenty, sugar, question is, who's talkin' and who's listenin'."

Vivian turned slightly toward her. "Always both," she said.

Frank flipped a page of the Tribune, the headline smudged by whiskey rings.

"Vega's still writing like she's got a grudge," he said.

Vivian smiled faintly. "She should. The city earns it."

The jukebox clicked, Springsteen's *Born to Run* crashing restlessly against the walls.

Nikki. Division Street. The trail just moved from rumor to map.

Vivian leaned back, cigarette curling smoke toward the ceiling. "Thanks, Ronnie," she said softly. "You've still got the best ear in the room."

Ronnie smirked—unsure if she'd won or been played.

***

11

SHADOWS

FRIDAY, NOVEMBER 14, 1975

"Ghosts don't haunt the dead, lass. They haunt the living."

Seamus's words trailed her out of the Rail—half warning, half benediction.

The El screamed overhead, sparks raining like fleeting stars. The warmth of the Rail was already a block behind her—traded for cold steel and echo.

Vivian walked steadily, breath misting in the dark. The night still carried Ronnie's perfume and Loretta's smoke, like a film she couldn't wash off.

Ronnie had dropped Nikki's name too easily. Not gossip, placement. And Eddie's stumble hadn't been nerves; it was guilt. Behind those kind eyes, something he'd seen or heard remained. She made a mental note to press him later, but gently. Decency like his cracked under pressure.

Halfway down Lake Street, the street changed tone. A train rumbled above, and she caught sight of movement across the tracks—a man and a woman standing in the wash of a streetlight near the curb. The man pulled his coat collar high and lowered his hat, hiding his features. Sculpted into a twist, the woman's hair caught the light, reflecting it perfectly.

The man leaned in and struck a match. The flare caught his profile for a moment. He cupped the flame to her cigarette, then shook the match out and dropped it in the gutter. The woman exhaled smoke through a practiced smile. They spoke briefly—too quietly for her to catch, then a yellow cab slid to the curb. Both climbed in, doors shutting in sequence, and the car pulled away toward Ashland.

Vivian watched the taillights vanish, the afterimage bleeding into the El's sparks. Something about the man's posture, the stillness in his movements, tugged at her memory. She couldn't place it—but she would.

When she reached the spot where they'd stood, she noticed something pale near the curb—a torn matchbook, damp but legible. She bent, flicking it open under the streetlight. Inside, a stamped logo: *Wellsford Hotel.* The same spot, the same gutter where the man had flicked his match away.

Too clean to be a coincidence.

She slipped it into her coat pocket, thumb brushing the raised print once before she moved on.

At her stoop, the new bulb Hal had fixed glowed warm over the dented mailboxes. She fished out her keys, brass cool against her glove. She'd thank him tomorrow—he liked that sort of thing, and she could afford the kindness.

Inside, the hallway smelled of dust and steam heat. Her apartment met her with its hush. She hung her coat and settled into the quiet. The night's armor gave way to skin.

She poured herself a cup of tea, steam rising softly against the dim light, and settled into her chair. From the table, the matchbook peeked out beside her notebook. She stared at it; the lamplight catching the logo, making it shimmer.

The man's silhouette tugged again at her mind—the deliberate stance, the shape of his jaw. The woman's hairstyle was too sculpted, too sure of itself. Both felt familiar, like faces glimpsed once too often in places you shouldn't have been.

Every case started the same way—one wrong name, one clue no one else cared about.

Outside, another train thundered past, rattling the windowpanes. She closed her eyes and let its rhythm settle her thoughts.

Tomorrow she'd start digging—City Hall records, maybe the Tribune, morgue or the public library. If Donna or Nikki's name showed up anywhere—missing persons, police blotter, society pages—she'd find it.

By Monday night, she'd know enough to walk into the Wellsford.

For now, the night was hers.

***

12

WEEKEND

SATURDAY–SUNDAY, NOVEMBER 15–16, 1975

Saturday came gray and thin through the blinds. Vivian lingered over coffee, notebook open, the words *Milwaukee Avenue—ankh—Nikki* underlined twice. The city was slow to wake, but she wasn't. The case had gone quiet, and she didn't trust quiet.

By midmorning she was at City Hall, the building that pretended to be honest. Fluorescent lights hummed over rows of metal file cabinets. A clerk in horn-rims barely looked up when she asked for missing-person reports from the past year.

"Plenty of those," he muttered, sliding her a stack thick as a phone book.

She flipped through the pages—runaways, overdoses, unclaimed bodies. *No Donna Mitchell or Nikki.* But names blurred into patterns, and patterns were what she lived on. A handful of entries listed *unidentified female, mid-twenties, 19th District.* She copied the case numbers into her notebook. Wrong files often hid the right stories.

A strand of hair fell across her cheek as she leaned in, eyes burning under the fluorescent glare. The silence close, the kind that waited for someone's mistake to show.

By afternoon, the stiff wind chasing her coat, she walked up the steps of the Chicago Public Library. The reading room smelled of dust and resolve. Down in the basement, the microfilm machines buzzed like insects. She scrolled through months of headlines—missing girls, vice raids, political scandals—until one column stopped her cold.

"Sheridan, M.—Tribune Foreign Desk, Saigon Bureau, 1969.

Her breath caught. Mick's byline."

Her pulse stuttered. She leaned closer, reading the last line aloud under her breath:"*Truth's the only country worth dying for.*"

The words hit harder than they should have. She touched the glass as if it might still be warm from his hands. Her reflection stared back—older, wearier, still enlisted. She smiled faintly, tracing his name on the screen before moving on.

Then, another headline a few months later caught her eye:

"Vice Division Scandal Tied to Prominent Chicago Figures—Investigator Margaret O'Connell Leads Inquiry."

Vivian froze. *Mags.*

She read the story twice. It described an internal corruption probe from 1966—an operation that had pulled in half the Vice Division and a "high-society madam" with political clients. A young detective named S. DeMarco helped to close the investigation. The photo below the fold showed Mags in her trench coat outside City Hall, jaw set, eyes cutting through the gray. Behind her, DeMarco stood half-turned to the camera—square jaw, heavy brow. The same silhouette she'd seen under the El.

The third paragraph buried the madam's name: Rosaline Marchand.

Vivian sat back, heart ticking slow. The man and woman by the streetlight hadn't been chance—they'd been ghosts walking in daylight. The memory of the match flare returned unbidden, the cigarette's brief halo. She could almost smell the smoke again.

By dusk, the weekend shifted—Sunday easing in on the smell of rain and fried dough drifting from Halsted. Vivian walked without hurry, collar turned up against the chill. Near the corner of Randolph she saw him again—Detective S. DeMarco, Vice Division—laughing with two girls too young for the makeup they wore. He slipped them folded bills, then glanced up, eyes meeting hers for one sharp second. Recognition flared, then calculation.

She kept walking, the sound of her boots swallowed by the rain, but the echo from the *Ashland case* followed her—his signature on the report that buried a witness, his grin when the file disappeared. And now, the photo. The same jaw, the same stillness.

Some rot never retires.

Back home, she set her notebook on the table. Under the last line—*Nikki—Division Street;* she added one more:

DeMarco—Vice Division—Marchand—Wellsford.

Outside, the rain began again, soft and steady. The El rattled overhead, iron heartbeat of the city. Vivian leaned back in her chair, listening.

The weekend gave her no answers, only direction—and a face she wouldn't forget.

Tomorrow, she'd start digging where the city kept its ghosts.

*****

13

DIVISION

MONDAY, NOVEMBER 17, 1975

Monday crept in gray and sour. Vivian let the radio drone while she poured coffee and watched the steam rise, the smell of burnt toast and chilly rain filling the room.

"City Hall denies any connection between the vice raids and the recent indictments ... " the announcer rasped. Then came another headline—missing evidence from the 19th District property room, a "network of payoffs" from precinct captains to aldermen.

Rot was the city's natural state. She shut the radio off mid-sentence.

At the table, her notebook sat open. Nikki—three times underlined. Beneath it: Division Street—start west, work east.

By early afternoon the clouds had thinned, but the wind still cut. She walked, the pulse underfoot—storefront radios, neon signs warming for night, the smell of roasted spices drifting from tavern doors.

The first pawnshop sat near Wood Street, window stacked with tarnished watches and guitars missing strings.

"Ever see her?" Vivian asked, sliding the photograph across the counter. Donna's calm face stared up, the ankh faint at her collar.

The owner squinted, shook his head. "Looks like one of them California girls. Try the record shop down the block—they get that crowd."

She did. The clerk barely looked up. Another shrug, another dead end. She kept east—one shop, then another, each with its own brand of indifference.

At a narrow jewelry-repair stall wedged between a barbershop and a diner, a woman in her fifties peered up from her bench magnifier.

"That picture," the woman said, tapping the photo. "I seen one like that. Girl had it on—brass-colored, with that same cross-loop thing."

Vivian's voice stayed even. "When?"

"Couple weeks back," the woman said. "Called herself Nikki. Thought about trading it—brass, cross-loop and all. Then she changed her mind. Said it was hers and no one else's. Left when two men came in—one I've seen working the door at the Vortex near Wells."

Vivian studied the photo once more, then slipped it back into her coat. "Thanks." She left ten on the counter.

For the first time, Nikki wasn't just a name in a notebook. She was flesh, breath, and regret. And she had the ankh.

A chill drew tight across Vivian's chest. *Donna wasn't coming back.* The truth sat cold, but clean. She'd learned to take her answers that way.

East down Division, the neon flickered alive, the street humming toward night. At the far end, the VORTEX sign sputtered red against the dusk—a heartbeat through haze.

Nightclubs were always a mirror of the city—bright, loud, and desperate to be seen. The Rail belonged to survivors; the Vortex to those still pretending they were free. She'd tried that once, a lifetime ago.

Vivian drew one last drag, flicked the cigarette away, and turned toward the El.

She'd be back after dark.

***

14

VORTEX

MONDAY, NOVEMBER 17, 1975

Monday night, and the city was restless again. The Vortex was already pulsing, bass thrumming through the pavement, a teal haze leaking from the doorway into the chill. From inside came the opening groove of The O'Jays' *For the Love of Money,* that relentless rhythm that made the floor vibrate like a heartbeat gone bad.

She paused outside, cigarette ember flaring as she studied her reflection in the window: a short black wrap dress, black gloves smooth at her wrists, black boots climbing high.

She smirked at her own audacity. Let them think she didn't belong. She wasn't here to belong—she was here to hunt. Black wasn't for charm; it was for control.

Inside, the air was thick with smoke and perfume. Colored lights swept the walls, painting everything in motion. The crowd was young—bare arms, vinyl skirts, laughter sharp as broken glass. Vivian threaded through them, her pace unhurried, every step deliberate.

10cc's *I'm Not in Love* drifted from the speakers next, soft and hypnotic, the song that blurred the line between longing and denial. The melody curled through the room, dissolving into the bass.

Heads turned. She caught the looks—curious, hungry, uncertain—and met them with a calm that dared them to look longer. Confidence wasn't a pose for her; it was armor polished to a shine. A few smiles lingered too long, half invitation, half dare. She gave them what they wanted: a glance, a curve of a smile, just enough to remind them she was something different—older, steadier, dangerous in a way they didn't understand.

At the bar, a young man in a denim vest leaned close before she even ordered. He couldn't hide the rush in his voice, the thrill of proximity.

"You don't come here often," he said, almost tripping over the words.

Vivian let her eyes travel slowly from his shoes to his mouth, then past him to the bartender. "Only when I have to," she said.

The bartender was maybe twenty-five, broad-shouldered, trying not to watch her.

"What can I get you?" he asked.

"Bourbon," Vivian said.

She let him pour, then rested her fingertips on the glass a moment longer than necessary—enough to make him wonder what that meant.

"Looking for a girl," she said. "Tall, long hair. Calls herself Nikki."

He hesitated, pretending not to know the name.

Vivian tilted her head. "Come on, sweetheart. You pour drinks for everyone in this place. Maybe she owes someone money. Maybe she owes you."

He cracked, just enough. "Back corner booth. Comes and goes. Never stays long."

Vivian said, "Thanks." Her smile didn't reach her eyes.

As she turned from the bar, she felt it before she saw it—eyes on her. A prickle at the base of her neck. She followed the feeling across the mirrored wall and froze.

Across the room, through the shifting teal light, a woman sat half-hidden in the corner booth. The hair was wrong—jet black, cut sharp, but the posture, the jawline, the careless confidence were unmistakable.

Then the light changed, catching on a small pendant at her throat.

The ankh.

Vivian felt the air thin around her. The hair didn't matter anymore. The pendant told her everything. Donna's ankh. Nikki's neck. Same gleam, same shape she'd traced in the photograph.

Movement caught at the edge of the mirror—two men at the far end of the bar, not drinking, just watching. Not the watching born of interest; theirs was the patient stillness of men on a job. One whispered to the other before their eyes slid away when she glanced up. Tail, not temptation.

Realization sparked, followed by a harder truth: she was looking at her younger self. The girl's vinyl outfit, bold and bright, was a style Vivian had once claimed as her own.

The echo landed too close, and she hated the way it felt.

Their eyes met in the mirror. Nikki's smile was small, knowing. She leaned toward the man beside her, said something, then looked straight at Vivian again.

The message was clear: *I see you, too.*

Nikki's lips shaped something else across the room—words half-lost in the pulse of the bass. Vivian read them anyway.

Vivian didn't move. She let the bass thrum through her; the bourbon burn down; her pulse steady. She saw herself in that girl—what she'd buried, what she'd outlived, what might have consumed her if she'd never learned control.

The bartender broke her trance with a low voice. "You okay, lady?"

Vivian turned back, a faint smile curving. "Never better."

When she looked again, Nikki was gone from the booth—but not from the mirror. Now she was in motion, weaving through the crowd, head half-turned, just enough for Vivian to catch the flash of the ankh under the strobe.

The hunter and the hunted, trading roles in a single breath.

Vivian finished her drink, left cash on the counter, and moved after her—slow, deliberate, every step cutting through the crowd's pulse until only the beat remained.

The crowd swallowed her, and somewhere ahead, a reflection moved that wasn't hers.

As the door thudded shut behind her, the music changed—David Bowie's *Fame* bursting through the walls, sharp and electric, echoing the truth both women now understood: in this city, everyone sold a piece of themselves.

***

15

NIKKI

The crowd thinned near the back, where the air turned heavy with smoke and low light. Vivian followed the shimmer of the ankh down a short corridor toward the lounge—a narrow space of booths and mirrors that caught every flash of blue and red like pulse beats.

Nikki waited in the last booth, one leg crossed over the other, cigarette burning slowly between her fingers. She looked up before Vivian could speak, a small, knowing smile curving at her mouth.

"You move fast," Vivian said.

Nikki tilted her head. "You follow well."

From the main floor, Donna Summer's *Love to Love You Baby* pulsed through the walls—low, rhythmic, and relentless, every breath and beat threading the smoke like a slow fuse. A few men drifted past, giving the two women a wide berth.

Vivian slid into the seat opposite. "I've been looking for you."

"I figured." Nikki tapped ash into an empty glass. "You've been asking around all day. That echoes."

Vivian's eyes flicked to the ankh glinting at her throat. "That belonged to Donna Mitchell."

Nikki didn't flinch. "She gave it to me."

Vivian let the words hang between them. "Why?"

"She said it didn't stand for what it used to." Nikki's tone softened, almost wistful. "Said I reminded her of someone she used to be. I tried to tell her the city doesn't leave room for that kind of nostalgia."

"You knew her," Vivian asked.

"Not well enough to save her," Nikki replied.

"You don't seem the saving type," said Vivian.

Nikki smiled faintly. "Neither do you."

For a moment, neither spoke. The light flickered, leaving them in the same dim glow—two women from different decades but bound by the same sharpened instincts. Vivian saw it clearly now: the poise, the calculation, the armor worn as skin. Nikki was what she might've become if she'd let go of truth and leaned fully into survival.

Nikki broke the silence first. "The Madam tried to bring me in. Figures a girl like me could double her profits. Some cops in Vice think the same. They all want a piece, but I don't belong to anyone."

"Hard way to live," Vivian said.

"It's the only way."

"DeMarco thinks he owns this city," Nikki mouthed. "Some of us stopped paying rent."

Vivian's brow lifted, just enough to answer: "You planning to move out?"

A flash of teeth. "Maybe. Maybe I'm just looking for the spare key."

Vivian leaned forward. "Donna—what happened?"

Nikki's eyes lowered, the veneer cracking for just a breath. "She was too soft. Thought she could love her way through it. The city eats girls like that." She crushed out her cigarette. "I told her to get out. She wouldn't listen."

The truth hit Vivian like cold air. The tone, the regret—it wasn't guilt. It was grief disguised as anger. "So you didn't—"

"Kill her?" Nikki finished. "No. But I watched her drown all the same."

The bass from the main room surged, shaking the mirrors. For an instant, Vivian saw their reflections blur into one—a double image, indistinguishable. The bass hit again, and for a blink, she couldn't tell which one of them was breathing.

Nikki stood, slinging her coat over her shoulder. "You're chasing ghosts, Kessler. Whatever's left of that girl, it's long gone."

Vivian rose, blocking her path. "You know who put her there."

Nikki's gaze steadied and measured. "Maybe. But knowing won't change a thing. You'll find that out soon enough." Nikki's head turned slightly toward the shadowed figures down the hall—as if to acknowledge, without words, the source.

She leaned close, voice dropping to a whisper that brushed Vivian's ear.

"If you want to know what really happened, don't look for the girls. Look for the ones who buy them."

Vivian turned toward the men, but Nikki was already gone—back into the pulse and smoke, swallowed by the crowd.

Vivian stood for a long moment, watching the space where Nikki had been. The mirror opposite caught her face and, for a fleeting second, Nikki's ghost beside it—two survivors separated only by purpose. For the first time, Vivian saw hesitation in that reflection—the kind that belonged to someone standing at the edge of a choice. *Whatever Nikki decided next, it wouldn't be for herself.*

Donna gave away the one charm she swore would keep her from getting lost. Maybe she already knew she was.

She knew now: Nikki wasn't the cause. Donna hadn't run. And the only way to end this was to confirm the stiff, to look the city's truth square in the face.

And she'd have to tell Peter. He'd clung to hope like a lifeline, and she was about to cut it. Even bourbon couldn't keep her warm now.

Vivian looked for the men once again and turned toward the exit, the music fading behind her, the ankh's shimmer still burning in her mind.

***

16

—·—

RECORDS

TUESDAY, NOVEMBER 18, 1975

Tuesday dawned brittle and gray. The jukebox sat silent; its neon buzz was weak against the daylight. The Rail was empty except for Eddie and Vivian—the rare hour when even the city seemed to pause.

Eddie sat two stools down, Tribune folded across the bar, reading more from habit than interest. His half-drunk coffee steamed between them.

Vivian's notebook lay open beside her own untouched cup. Her pen traced slow circles around a single line: *Confirm the stiff.*

"Quiet morning," Eddie said without looking up. "You can learn a lot in quiet," she replied.

She wore the cognac dress, with short sleeves that caught the gray light, a belt cinched sharply at the waist, and gloves smooth against the rim of her cup. With intent, she chose every detail. She knew exactly how that dress would play on Callahan's nerves—how to loosen him without a word.

Eddie finally folded the paper and set it aside. "You heading out somewhere?" She took a sip of cold coffee. "I've got a few things to settle."

He hesitated, eyes fixed on the steam curling from his cup. "Viv... there's something I should've said earlier."

She looked up, waiting.

"It was a couple of nights ago, after the soldier kid came in." He trailed off, shrugging. "You know how she gets. Ronnie's got a way of making a man think twice before crossing her."

Vivian's expression didn't change. "So you thought silence was safer."

Eddie nodded, shame flickering behind his eyes. "Didn't seem important then. Guess it was."

"It was," she sighed. "But you're telling me now. That's what matters."

He gave a small uncertain smile, like a boy who'd been forgiven but wasn't sure why.

She closed her notebook and met his eyes. "Eddie, I'm counting on you to keep an ear open, not a mouth."

"Sure, Viv. Always."

She smiled—polite, not warm. "Good."

When she stood, the stool creaked against the tile, the sound small and final. Eddie watched her go, then turned back to the paper, pretending to read.

She'd phoned ahead, a quiet promise that she only needed five minutes. By the time she reached the precinct, the morning had turned hard and thin.

Callahan waited near the side entrance, cigarette burning low between his fingers. He spotted her from halfway down the block and waved her closer, eyes darting up and down the street.

"Keep it quick," he muttered. "Shift changes in ten. If anyone sees me letting you in, I'm cooked."

Vivian gave a small, knowing smile. "Then don't get seen."

He looked tired, wary—a man already rehearsing his excuses.

"You shouldn't be here, Viv. I told you last time—let this one lie."

She stepped closer, the muted sheen of her cognac dress catching what little light leaked through the overcast. The scent of her perfume mingled with his smoke.

"Not here for trouble," she whispered. "Just the truth."

He tried to hold his ground, eyes skimming the hallway instead of her. "Truth's a slippery thing in this place."

"Then hold it still for me."

Something in her tone—or maybe the calm precision of the way she wore that dress—made his resistance falter. He took one last drag, ground out the cigarette, and unlocked the side door.

Inside, their footsteps echoed down corridors that smelled of smoke and disinfectant. Phones rang faintly from deeper offices. Callahan kept glancing over his shoulder, half expecting a captain to appear. From somewhere down the hall, a transistor radio crackled—The Eagles' *Lyin' Eyes*.

"You never make this easy," he muttered.

"That's why you called me once," she said.

He gave a short, defeated nod and led her to a steel door stamped **RECORDS—AUTHORIZED PERSONNEL ONLY.** The door sat next to another marked **VICE EVIDENCE—RESTRICTED ACCESS.** Both doors bore new key-card locks, red lights glowing faintly above the handles, security upgrades that said everything about what the city feared might leak.

"I shouldn't be doing this," Callahan said, quieter now.

"You already did," she replied.

He opened the records room, flicked on the light, found and handed her a folder marked **Unidentified Female—November 2, 1975.**

Vivian opened the folder. The paperwork was thin: one photograph, an inventory sheet, a coroner's summary typed on yellowing paper. Her eyes moved quickly until a line near the bottom brought her to a dead stop: *Distinctive mark: small blue tattoo behind right ear, star shape.*

Peter had mentioned it once—how Donna came back from California "with a tiny star she said would keep her from getting lost."

Vivian's throat tightened. The words blurred. There was nobody left to see; the file told her everything.

"Overdose," Callahan said. "With signs of assault. Vice called it accidental. File got buried the same week the indictments started flying."

Vivian closed the folder. "You going to tell me who signed it?"

He hesitated. "You don't want that list, Viv."

"Sure, I do."

He gave a humorless smile. "You never learn."

"Maybe I do," she said. "I just don't like what it teaches me."

She looked back down at the folder, forcing herself to read the last lines.

Disposition: Interred—Cook County Cemetery (Potter's Field), November 5, 1975, Case 75-1127, Section 9, Row 3.

She copied the numbers into her notebook slowly and steadily. A place to stand—at least that much she could give them.

Then, above the stamped signature, another name caught her eye: *Detective S. DeMarco—Vice Division.*

The second time seeing that name in connection with a buried case made the pattern undeniable. It wasn't a coincidence—it was proof. DeMarco wasn't just another dirty cop; he was the thread running through the city's rot.

Vivian shut the folder. The click of the metal clasp was loud in the quiet.

"Thank you, Tommy," she said finally, her tone softening, almost flirtatious. "You've got more backbone than most men in this building. Maybe I'll buy you a drink sometime—off the record." He looked at her, unsure if she meant it.

As she passed him, the heel of her boot brushed his shoe—light, deliberate, just enough to pull his breath short.

Vivian smiled faintly. "Keep your head down, Jack."

Outside, the wind cut hard from the lake. She lit a cigarette, the flame trembling in the breeze. Smoke curled and vanished almost instantly.

Donna Mitchell was dead. The city had chewed her up and buried the rest under paperwork and lies.

Vivian drew one more drag, exhaled slowly. She knew what came next.

She'd have to tell Peter.

He'd been holding on to hope like it was oxygen, and she was about to take that from him. But better the truth than a ghost. Always tell the truth.

She dropped the cigarette, watched it die against the wet pavement, and turned toward the bus stop. The day was just beginning, but it already felt like night.

***

17

—·—

GONE

TUESDAY, NOVEMBER 18, 1975

Tuesday evening settled in wet and gray. Rain streaked the windows, blurring the neon reflection of the sign outside.

At the Lake Street Grill, Vivian paused at the door before stepping in. She'd chosen her most protective leather armor—a dark, structured jacket with clean lines and no flash. Not allure this time—just something to hold her together.

Peter was already there, sitting in the same booth where they'd met days ago. His coffee was cold, untouched. He looked up as she approached, eyes dull, like someone who already knew the answer but hoped the words might change it.

"Thanks for coming," he said.

Vivian slid into the booth across from him, setting her notebook gently on the table.

"You wanted answers," she breathed. "I've them."

He nodded, fingers tightening around his cup. "Go ahead."

She didn't rush. Her voice was low, even. Some truths were better delivered like wounds—clean, no hesitation.

"I confirmed it through the coroner's file," she said. "The body the police listed as unidentified, it's Donna."

For a heartbeat, she couldn't look at him. The words hung in the air like smoke that wouldn't clear. She struck a match, let it burn to her fingers, then dropped it. *So this is what silence costs,* she thought.

Peter blinked hard. "You're sure?"

Vivian hesitated just long enough to soften the blow. "There's no doubt. The file lists a small blue tattoo behind her right ear—a star."

Peter stared past her, his jaw trembling. "She said she got that out in California. My mother hated it."

His breath caught. "So that's it. She's gone."

Vivian reached across the table, laid her gloved hand on his arm. She didn't speak. She just stayed there, still and steady, letting the silence stretch.

After a long while, Peter whispered, "It doesn't seem real."

"I know," she said softly.

He looked up, eyes wet. "I kept thinking she'd walk through that door, you know? Just walk in like it never happened."

Vivian's voice stayed calm, measured. "The city doesn't give that kind of mercy. But she's at rest now. Potter's Field, Section Nine. I made sure you'd have the record."

He nodded slowly, then looked away. "My parents—they'll need to know. They'll want to... I don't know. Visit, maybe."

He rubbed his eyes. "They said a detective called a couple of weeks ago—DeMarco, I think. Said her case was closed, but he was vague. I thought it was just another cop trying to clear his desk."

Vivian's expression didn't change, but her mind sharpened at the name. DeMarco again. She filed it away without a word.

Peter exhaled shakily. "I don't know if I can come back from this."

Vivian squeezed his arm gently through the glove. "You will. Just not tonight."

He managed a nod, slid from the booth, and stood there a moment before speaking. "I should go tell them. They've been waiting for something I can't give them."

She reached into her bag, the photo between her fingers. "You should take this," she said.

Peter shook his head. "Keep it. You'll make better sense of her than I ever could."

She didn't look at it until he was gone. The image stared up—Donna frozen in the sunlight of a summer that never came back.

She didn't stop him. Just watched as he walked out into the mist, shoulders hunched against the cold.

When the door closed behind him, the diner felt hollow. Vivian stayed seated, staring at the window where the rain cut the neon into crooked lines. She thought of Mags—the steadiness in her voice, the way she'd once said, *Truth doesn't heal fast, Viv. But it's the only thing that does.*

Vivian gathered her notes, slipped them back into her bag, and stood. The leather creaked softly as she moved—a quiet armor against the ache that lingered.

Outside, the rain met her face like ash. She drew her coat tight and walked into the city's hum—tired, restless, unrepentant.

***

18

—·—

LINE

Hours later, back in her apartment, the rain clung to the windows, turning the city's glow into streaks of dull gold—like film grain caught in motion. Vivian sat in her living room, lights low, wrapped in the quiet hum of the building.

Her coat hung over the chair, boots by the door. She wore only a man's white shirt, with bare legs folded beneath her. No armor tonight—just skin and air.

The old camera sat on the shelf above the table, dust veiling the lens. She hadn't touched it since Mick's last assignment, but the sight of it steadied her—the only lens that ever told the truth.

A drink waited on the table beside her open notebook, untouched. At the center of the page, a single name—DeMarco—circled twice.

For a while, she just stared at it. Then at the rain. Then at nothing.

Her thoughts drifted to Peter's face, the hollow sound of his voice when he said he didn't know if he'd recover. To the look she'd seen in other rooms, other years, when the truth landed like a brick.

And then to Mick—the day the Tribune called, the man in the gray suit who couldn't meet her eyes when he said the jungle had taken him. That same silence now belonged to Peter—the sound of loss learning its own name.

She rubbed her temples, eyes closed. "So, this is it," she muttered to the empty room. "This is all there is."

But Mags's voice surfaced—steady, the way it always had in the critical years.

"*You can't fix the city, Viv. You can only make it answer for one lie at a time.*"

Vivian exhaled through her nose, slowly and deliberate. That was Mags—never dramatic, never cruel, just right. Always right.

And Mags was still right. Vivian reached for her notebook again, flipped to a clean page, and wrote in tight, slanted letters:

Find the Madam—who protects her.

She tapped the pen twice against the paper, then added below it:

DeMarco—Vice Division.

Nikki's voice drifted back, smoke and warning braided together: *Don't look for the girls. Look for the ones who buy them.*

Vivian sat back, the reflection washing over her like a tide. In the glass, her face merged with the lights outside—half shadow, half glow.

She thought of the men who kept the Madam safe—politicians, cops, maybe even a judge or two. It had always protected its own rot. That part would never change.

But she didn't have to let it define her. Or break her.

She closed the notebook, placed it on the table, and leaned back into the silence. For a moment, it felt almost peaceful—the space between storms.

Outside, the rain eased. The El rumbled past, carrying the city's pulse through another sleepless night.

***

19

PART III—GLASS AND FIRE

"There's no clean money in a dirty town. You just learn whose dirt you can live with."—Seamus

***

20

POTTER'S FIELD

WEDNESDAY, NOVEMBER 19, 1975

She was at Potter's Field by Wednesday morning, the cold biting through her gloves before she'd even stepped from the cab. The radio hummed through static—Fleetwood Mac's *Landslide.* Stevie Nicks asked if time made you bolder as the city rolled past. Vivian didn't answer.

She pulled the fare from her purse—five bucks, more than it should've cost—and told the driver to keep the change.

Coat collar high, boots crunching against frozen dirt, she scanned the field that stretched wide and colorless beneath a sky the color of unpolished tin. The place smelled of rain and rust, like something the city had buried too deep to name.

Beyond the fence, the highway emitted a faint trace of another radio, with Aerosmith's *Dream On* fading into static just before the chorus. The wind carried it off like a memory that refused to rest.

She carried a folded scrap of paper with Donna's case number—Section 9, Row 3.

The file had given her the facts. The ground would give her the truth.

A man in a city parka stood near a maintenance shed, gray hair slicked to his scalp, cigarette trembling between fingers gone to ash.

"Whatcha looking for?" he asked.

She handed him the note.

He read it twice, slower the second time, then looked up. "You Kessler?"

"Used to be."

He nodded, more in recognition than surprise. "Harlan Bates," he said, offering the name like an afterthought. "Used to be CPD maintenance detail—Town Hall back in the day. I remember your picture from the Ashland case. Hell of a mess."

Vivian's mouth twitched faintly. "They all were. That one just made the papers."

Bates crushed his cigarette under his heel and started walking, shovel clinking against his boot. "Come on. They sent her here quiet," he said. "Truck came in the rain. No tag, no family. Just a file from Vice."

"DeMarco's signature?"

He gave a humorless laugh. "His and three others. Same month—early November. All girls about the same age. All 'unidentified.' Back then I thought it was sloppy work. Now I know it's worse. Every year the cover-ups get cleaner, the ground a little fuller."

They passed rows of leaning stakes and sunken mounds. The wind caught at the edges of his words. "We used to keep tags on the sticks," he said. "Helps when folks come looking. Lately, they tell us to leave 'em blank. 'Budget cuts,' they say."

He spat into the dirt. "Truth gets cheaper every year."

They stopped at a low mound marked by a bent iron rod. No flowers, no sign of care—only a number scratched faint into a rusted plate.

"This one's hers," Bates said. "At least it was. Paperwork gets fuzzy after they start moving 'em around. Makes it tidy for the records. Spring rains took the tag off that row."

He looked down the line. "She came in a couple weeks ago—early November. Night shift. I remember because De-Marco brought another girl the same run—same precinct, same story. You'd think the ground would be full by now, but somehow there's always room."

Vivian kneeled, gloved fingers tracing the frozen soil. The earth felt harder here, newer. "How many others?"

"Too many," he said. "But I stopped counting when the brass stopped caring. City's rotting from the inside, and the stink's the only thing they still cover up."

Silence settled heavily enough to bend the wind.

She rose slowly. "You kept quiet."

He met her eyes. "Didn't seem to matter back then. You dig long enough in this town, you think the dirt's the cleanest part."

Vivian reached into her purse, pulled out a ten. He waved it off.

"Keep it. Just... whatever you're chasing, don't end up here."

She nodded once—more oath than thanks—and looked out over the rows.

To the east, she noted a half-collapsed elm and a rusted drainage pipe jutting from the hill. Landmarks enough for Peter to find the place later, if he needed to see for himself.

As she turned to leave, the wind tore through the field, flattening brittle grass. The rows blurred together, numbers without faces, stories without endings. Chicago's quiet ledger of forgotten souls.

They buried Donna, but not the men whose signatures had helped erase her.

And now she had more than grief—she had a name, a date, and a witness.

She knew exactly where to dig next.

***

21

MADAM

WEDNESDAY, NOVEMBER 19, 1975

By early evening she was back at The Rail, the chill from Potter's Field still clinging to her coat. Six days since Peter had walked through the door, and the city was finally answering back.

The bar sat between lives—too early for the night crowd, too late for the day's last drunks. Neon leaked through the windows in tired streaks; Al Green murmured *For the Good Times.*

Eddie read her silence, slid a bourbon across the bar. She took it neat.

Loretta arrived with the wind—trench damp, scarf tight.

She dropped onto the next stool, lit a cigarette, and studied Vivian's reflection in the mirror.

"You've been stirring puddles again."

"Trying to see what floats," Vivian said.

Loretta smirked. "Careful—some things float because they're rotten."

Vivian set her glass down. "I found something on my way home the other night right by my alley. A matchbook in the gutter. Paper shouldn't survive long there, but this one was still clean enough to read."

Loretta's eyes narrowed; smoke slipped from the corner of her mouth. "What was on it?"

"Wellsford Hotel," Vivian said. "Figured that wasn't chance."

Loretta let out a low, knowing laugh. "Guess subtlety's wasted on you."

She reached into her coat and pulled out a fresh matchbook, a lipstick kiss pressed across the cover.

"Wellsford Hotel," she said again. "Ask for Madame Rosaline. Don't use her last name unless you want company."

Vivian turned the matchbook once between her fingers. "You sure?"

"Very." Loretta's voice dropped to a dry rasp. "She runs her girls like a stable—keeps a type for every man's lie. A dark one who can silence a room with a look, and a redhead mean enough to start a fire just to see who runs. The Madam likes her stories vivid."

Vivian slipped the matchbook into her coat. "Then she and I will get along fine."

"Don't thank me," Loretta said, eyes hard. "Just dig careful. The ground's full of men who thought they could hide forever."

Vivian finished her drink, left cash on the bar, and rose. "Then it's time to see what clean looks like."

Outside, the rain waited. The same logo burned warm in her pocket—no longer a coincidence, but a summons.

The city never handed out invitations. When it did, they were usually written in someone else's blood.

***

22

Callahan's Door

Wednesday, November 19, 1975

An hour after leaving The Rail, she was at Town Hall. Again, the rain started—steady but soft.

The precinct looked different after dark. A half-glow made every wall feel closer, the lights humming low. The day shift was gone, leaving only the smell of cigarettes, sweat, and yesterday's brew.

Vivian slipped through the side door—the one Callahan often forgot to lock. Her heels struck tile in slow rhythm, a sound the building still remembered.

He was in his office, sleeves rolled, tie loose, a single lamp spilling over a mess of papers—half reports, half alibis. He didn't look up right away.

"You never learned when to quit, Viv," he said finally, voice flat but softer than it should've been.

"Quitting's never been my line of work."

He rubbed a hand over his jaw, watching her cross the room. "You shouldn't be here. Not today."

"Then you should've locked the door."

She set the Wellsford matchbook on his desk, red lipstick marks up. "Recognize it?"

He stared at it, jaw tightening. "You've been busy."

"Potter's Field," she said. "DeMarco's name showed up again—same file, same signature. Still want to call it a coincidence?"

Callahan exhaled through his nose, slow. "You don't know what you're digging into."

Vivian leaned forward, the lamplight catching the edge of her jacket—the one he'd once called her armor. "I'm already in it, Tommy. The dirt's up to my knees."

He hesitated, eyes flicking from her face to the matchbook. The tension wasn't new—it had a history. She could feel him reaching for excuses he didn't believe.

"Viv, these people—"

"Are your people," she cut in.

That landed. His eyes flashed—the look that wanted to fight but had already lost.

Vivian sat, one leg over the other. She adjusted her heel against his desk, the scrape on wood small but steady. Control reclaimed.

Callahan's eyes flicked down, then up again. He swallowed hard. "You always knew how to make a point."

"I'm making one now," she said. "Who's behind the Wellsford? Who's keeping the Madam clean?"

He hesitated, jaw tightening before he spoke. "Vice Division runs it. DeMarco's their errand boy. But it doesn't stop there. The Madam's got aldermen, businessmen—hell, a captain or two—in her pocket. They keep her safe. She keeps them quiet."

Vivian didn't blink. "How deep are you in it?"

"I'm not," he said, too fast. Then quieter: "Not anymore."

He wasn't clean, just trying to remember how that felt.

"Then dig your way out. Who holds the ledger?"

Callahan rubbed his temple. "The Wellsford's a front. Money moves through Marquette Trust. Vice locks the files. You want them, you'll need DeMarco's key."

He looked up, guilt flattening his voice. "You're already on their list, Viv. They know you've been asking."

She rose, movements calm and deliberate. "Then they should've buried me deeper."

A shadow passed across the glass—too still, too deliberate. Callahan stiffened. "We're not alone."

He slid the matchbook into a drawer. "Back stairwell. Go."

She didn't move. "You going to keep cleaning up their mess, or finally make one of your own?"

His jaw set. "Get out while you can."

She stepped closer, boots silent, the chill of the air filling the space between them. "I've never been good at getting out, Tommy. Only through."

Then she was gone—down the side hall, her silhouette fading through flickering light and the smell of old coffee.

Outside, rain slicked the street, precinct windows glowing weak behind her. Vivian lit a cigarette, watching her reflection in a parked cruiser's window. Smoke curled, thin and certain.

If they wanted her quiet, it should've buried her deeper.

The rain hissed against the street, steady now, whispering over the cruiser's chrome. She drew one last drag, thinking of the way Callahan's resolve had cracked—not from fear, but from familiarity. That kind of sway wouldn't work on the Madam. Charm and history had their limits. The next move would need armor that left no doubt—black.

***

23

WELLSFORD

WEDNESDAY, NOVEMBER 19, 1975

The rain had stopped, but the streets still gleamed like wet glass. The city's night reflected itself in the puddles—neon, shadow, memory.

Vivian stepped out of the cab and paused beneath the Wellsford's flickering marquee. Four stories of limestone loomed above her, the building still pretending to be grand long after it had sold the act.

She'd dressed for it—black leather cut close, built for silence. Beneath it, a dark silk blouse traced the line of her throat, the buttons neat and deliberate. Her skirt was narrow enough to demand purpose in every step. Her boots gleamed—polished to mirror the city's filth back at itself.

Brown let her move through the city's seams unseen; black told the city she'd stopped running. The brown was for work; the black was for war.

Inside, the Wellsford smelled of perfume and plaster dust. The chandeliers hung like weary bones, and the carpet—once crimson—had faded to the color of dried blood. A clerk straightened when she entered but didn't speak. He pressed a buzzer and nodded toward the side elevator. No questions.

The elevator hummed upward, slow as guilt. Vivian's reflection ghosted back at her in the steel door—eyes clear, mouth set, her silhouette catching every flicker of light.

The third-floor corridor stretched long and narrow, portraits of women lining the walls—painted smiles from better decades. Each one watched as she passed.

At the end of the hall, a young woman in sequins waited, smile too wide to be real. "Madame Marchand is expecting you," she said, opening the door with a polished hand.

The room inside was warm, golden, dangerous. Lamplight softened the corners; the scent of brandy mingled with powder and lilies.

Madame Rosaline Marchand sat behind a lacquered desk near the window, every inch of her a study in control. Her hair was black, glossy as onyx, parted clean and pinned into a smooth chignon that caught the lamplight like oil on water. A whisper of amber and smoke drifted with her movements—the scent filling the room the way power does, without asking permission.

She wore ivory silk, high-collared, with pearl buttons glinting under the lamp. The fabric reflected light; Vivian's black absorbed it. Between them, power found two faces—one armored, one perfumed.

"Miss Kessler," Rosaline said, voice smooth as poured liquor. "You found us."

Vivian didn't sit. "It wasn't hard. Your name's been drifting through too many terrible stories."

Rosaline smiled. "People love stories. Especially the ones that make women villains."

"I don't deal in fiction."

"No," Rosaline replied, pouring herself a drink. "You sell truth. I sell relief. Both have their costs."

She let the glass turn in her hand, gaze steady. "Men in uniform, men in suits—it makes no difference. They all come knocking when the night runs out of mercy."

Vivian moved closer, unbuttoning her gloves with quiet precision. "DeMarco's your collector."

The Madam's eyes flickered. "You've been busy."

"I've been thorough."

Rosaline tilted her head, lamplight sliding along her black hair. "Careful. Thorough women disappear."

Vivian's tone didn't waver. "You've got girls all over this city. One of them calls herself Nikki."

Rosaline's smile barely moved. "Ah, the imitators. They come and go. I don't keep what won't kneel."

"Then you've seen her."

"I see everyone eventually, Miss Kessler."

She set her glass down with a soft click and studied Vivian for a long beat before smiling again, smaller, sharper. "You remind me of two of mine, once. A dark one who commands a room just by breathing. A redhead who burns it down when she's ignored."

Vivian's eyes narrowed. "That supposed to mean something?"

Rosaline leaned back, letting the light find the silk at her throat. "Only that every woman here starts with fire. Some keep it. Some get used to the smoke."

The line hung between them—provocation disguised as philosophy. Vivian saw it for what it was: bait. Rosaline was testing her, measuring where the cracks might show.

"Ambition's not what gets them killed," Vivian whispered.

Rosaline's smile curved, knowing. "No. It's believing they can win."

For a moment, silence settled—two operators pretending to sip tea.

"Donna Mitchell worked for you," Vivian said.

The Madam's gaze didn't falter. "She thought she could love her way through the world. The world doesn't love back."

"She ended up in Potter's Field."

Rosaline's voice softened, almost wistful. "So did I, once." She paused, eyes distant for the first time. "Difference is, I learned how to stay above ground."

Her hand trembled as she reached for the cigarette, just once, before the mask settled back into place. "In this city, survival's the only virtue left," she said. "The rest is décor."

A shadow shifted behind the curtain—broad-shouldered, waiting.

"You should go," Rosaline said. "The men you've angered prefer their ghosts quiet." She poured another drink and set it beside Vivian. "For courage, dear. You'll need it when you leave."

Vivian pulled on her gloves. "If courage came in glasses, you'd be out of business."

She turned toward the door. Rosaline's voice followed, smooth and amused. "Tell Callahan to stop sending apologies. I trade only in cash."

Vivian paused, looked back once. The lamplight caught both women in the mirror—one framed in white silk, the other swallowed by black. For an instant, they looked almost the same.

Then Vivian stepped into the hall. The air felt thinner now. Behind her, the door clicked shut, and the golden light dimmed to a slit beneath it.

She stood there a moment, breathing in the quiet, the hallway empty but for her reflection in a framed portrait—shadowed figure, pale face, eyes sharp with new understanding.

Outside, the Wellsford's neon flickered once, steadying into a dull red glow, reflected in the glass at the end of the corridor. Vivian lit a cigarette, her reflection ghosting in the rain-dark pane.

Rosaline had wanted to rattle her—and maybe she had, for a heartbeat. A dark one. A redhead. Two ghosts she didn't know yet, already stirring.

Vivian drew a slow drag, smoke curling and flattening against the low ceiling of the corridor.

"Nice try, Madam."

***

24

TRAP

WEDNESDAY, NOVEMBER 19, 1975

The elevator doors refused to open.

Vivian pressed the button once, then twice. Nothing. She turned back down the corridor, away from the elevator, stopping near the mirrored panel where a hairline fracture split her reflection.

The hallway stretched out again—Rosaline's suite at one end, the stairwell partway down, the air between them heavy with perfume and silence.

A small pause, breath tight in her chest. Not fear, calculation. Mags's voice, steady as always: *Control's not the absence of fear, it's what you do with it.*

They'd been waiting.

The corridor stretched quietly and too long. The portraits of women lining the walls seemed to watch her again, patient and knowing. At the far end, a shadow shifted—broad-shouldered, deliberate. Another silhouette lingered near the stairwell, not blocking it, just watching, waiting to see which way she moved.

Everything stopped talking. Rosaline was right.

Vivian turned, her coat moving like punctuation, and walked toward the stairs. Her heels struck the carpet with a steady, unhurried rhythm. Control was the only weapon that mattered. Mags had taught her that.

Halfway down, the stairwell lights flickered, slicing the air into slivers of light and dark. From somewhere above, a bass line seeped through the plaster—Barry White's *You're the First, the Last, My Everything.* Too sweet for the moment, its warmth twisted into something hollow as it echoed down the stairwell. The love song kept time with the danger closing in.

The footsteps behind her were soft—measured, professional. Two men, maybe three.

The second-floor door creaked below. Someone was waiting.

Vivian felt trapped.

A dull clatter echoed from the landing below—metal striking concrete, abrupt, like a struggle cut short. Vivian froze, breath held. Another sound followed—heels, light and deliberate, moving against the rhythm of the men above. Then stillness, as if the stairwell itself were listening.

Then—a voice from the shadows below: "You're not as quiet as you think."

Vivian froze. That tone. Smooth, amused.

A figure stepped into the stairwell. Vinyl jacket. Black hair loose, catching the weak light. Nikki.

"You shouldn't have come here," Nikki said. "They're already cleaning up."

"I'm not theirs to clean."

Nikki tilted her head. "Everyone's someone's mess."

Vivian almost smiled. Rosaline had said something like that, too. Maybe survival came from knowing when to be someone's problem, not their prize.

The door above slammed open. Heavy footsteps descended. Vivian's eyes moved—one sweep of the stairwell, one breath to count angles, timing, exits.

"Which side are you on?" Vivian asked.

"Tonight?" Nikki reached into her pocket and tossed a ring of keys. Metal struck Vivian's glove, cold and solid. "Laundry level. Back door. They won't chase you outside. Too many witnesses."

A bit surprised, Vivian asked, "Why help me?"

"Call it professional courtesy. And maybe I want to see who they send next time."

The voices above grew louder—gruff, impatient. Vivian watched the stairwell light pulse with each approaching step. Then she smiled, just enough.

"Follow my lead, Nikki," she whispered.

Nikki arched a brow but didn't argue.

Vivian seized the loose railing and yanked it until the metal screamed. The sound tore through the stairwell, echoing like an alarm.

The men stopped short, startled by the noise. Vivian waited for the hesitation—the one heartbeat of confusion, then said quietly, "Now."

They moved fast and silently, heels skimming concrete, breath measured. The commotion above bought them seconds—just enough.

By the time the nearest man reached the next landing, the women were gone.

Down one flight, then another—the air turned damp and close, thick with the scent of dust and detergent. A flickering bulb marked the basement door. Nikki shoved it open, and the night spilled in.

Rain hit like applause—sharp, relentless, without a trace of mercy. The alley stretched wide and wet, framed by the glow of a distant streetlight.

Vivian exhaled, the scent of perfume still clinging to her coat. It mixed with the city's rot, turning something once elegant into a warning. Her pulse was steady, not from calm but precision.

When she looked up, Nikki was already backing away, vinyl gleaming under the drizzle.

"We're even," Nikki said. "Next time, you're on your own."

"You could walk away from this," Vivian told her.

Nikki smiled faintly. "I did. You just walked in."

Then she was gone—vanishing between the buildings, swallowed by the city's damp breath.

Vivian looked down at the keys in her hand. One key had an engraved plate that read: VICE EVIDENCE–PROPERTY ROOM.

She turned it over once, feeling its weight, its promise. *Nikki, the dark one, just as Rosaline said?*

Which meant the redhead was still out there.

She flicked ash into the puddle. The rain hissed back.

The city wasn't done with her—never was.

***

25

Aftermath

Thursday, November 20, 1975

Late Thursday night, the Brass Rail was near empty when Vivian came in. Rain trailed her like a rumor, coat heavy, gloves still damp. The jukebox was dark for once, its silence louder than the trains clattering above.

She paused near the door, eyes adjusting to the half-light. For an instant, she thought she saw movement in the back booth—a flash of red hair catching the neon. Her pulse ticked once, then steadied. Just a waitress clearing glasses—wrong coat, hair too short. The city playing its tricks again.

Eddie looked up from behind the bar, mouth half-open to speak, but whatever words he had died at the sight of her. She didn't need questions. He didn't need answers. He slid her a glass before she asked. Bourbon—neat.

Seamus sat in his usual spot, haloed by the last weak glow from the Schlitz sign. Frank was a shadow two stools down, cigarette burning slow. Both men watched without watching.

Vivian set the keys on the bar. The tag caught the light: **VICE EVIDENCE—PROPERTY ROOM.**

Eddie's hand froze mid-wipe. Seamus leaned just enough to read it, eyes narrowing.

Eddie glanced at the tag, then down the bar.

"Jesus, Father..."

Seamus didn't look up. "So," he said softly, "you went digging where they told you not to."

Vivian nodded once. "Found what the city tried to forget."

She took a sip. The whiskey burned just enough to feel real.

"DeMarco?" Frank asked, voice low.

"Still breathing," she said. "For now."

Frank nodded once, then glanced at the keys. "How'd you come by those, Viv?"

She turned the glass in her hand, the bourbon catching the light. "A friend tossed them my way."

"Friend?" Seamus asked, skepticism in his drawl.

Vivian's mouth curved faintly. "Let's call her that for now."

The men didn't press. Some ghosts were better left unnamed.

The bar fell silent. Only the hum of old neon filled the gap. Outside, thunder rolled somewhere over the lake—a low growl that never reached the ground.

Seamus lifted his glass in a half-salute. "Told you, lass—the truth bites back."

Vivian met his eyes. "It missed the vein."

He smiled through his beard. "A near thing, then."

She didn't smile back. She just looked down at the keys, proof, leverage, a reason to keep breathing. It was also a promise—that the next truth she uncovered might finally draw blood.

It would keep lying. The men would use money to silence them. But the chain had cracked now, and that was enough for tonight.

She stood, leaving half her drink behind. The bar's light painted her in gold and shadow. She pulled on her gloves.

Eddie's voice caught her at the door. "You done with it, Viv?"

She paused, with one hand on the frame. "Done's not a word this city believes in."

The wind slipped through the open door, carrying rain and steel from the tracks above. She stepped out into it, head high, coat collar raised.

Behind her, Seamus murmured to no one in particular. "Still standing," he said. "So maybe it missed the vein after all."

The jukebox clicked to life on its own, unprompted—Dinah Washington, *This Bitter Earth*.

Vivian didn't look back. The street swallowed her silhouette, and the night kept its secrets.

***

26

—·—

PART IV—THE LONG MORNING

"Grace doesn't erase the stain. It just lets you see it and keep walking."—Seamus

***

27

Choice

Friday, November 21, 1975

Morning woke gray and tired on Friday, November 21, 1975.

Light leaked through the blinds in thin, uneven lines, slowly tracing the edge of the Formica table. The Vice Evidence key lay where she'd left it, catching that first scrap of morning as if waiting its turn to be judged.

Vivian sat across from it, one hand resting on her open notebook, the other holding a slice of toast gone cold. She bit into it absently, the taste of butter and burned edge grounding her more than coffee ever could. She hadn't written a word since Potter's Field. Some truths didn't need ink.

WGN droned low from the Zenith—talk of indictments, unnamed officers, an "ongoing internal review." The announcer's optimism was the kind only people behind desks could afford. She turned the volume down until it was barely a whisper.

Outside, the El rattled past, its rhythm running through the walls like background music. The sound was steady, almost comforting—a heartbeat she'd learned to live by.

Her eyes drifted to the key again, then to the old camera on the shelf. Mick's Leica. The lens cracked at the rim, just like the one that returned from Saigon. She remembered the way he used to chase light the way she chased truth—headlines, bodies, aftermaths. Once, in the Tribune darkroom, he'd shown her a print of an alderman shaking hands with a man already under indictment.

"The trick," he'd said, "is knowing when to stop developing. Let the shadows tell the rest."

The papers were printing unknown names now—different men, same rot. Mick would've known where to aim the lens. He always did until the jungle turned the viewfinder into a target.

She took a long sip of coffee gone lukewarm. Peter's face came back to her—the hollow stare across the diner booth, the tremor in his voice when hope finally broke. She'd seen that look before: wives waiting at pay phones, mothers clutching dog tags, sons looking for sisters already lost. It was the part of the job no one paid for, the weight that came after the answers.

Somewhere in the city, a dark-haired girl was still walking the edges—too smart to come home, too proud to disappear completely. Vivian hoped she'd keep moving; ghosts were safer that way.

Sometimes she thought about walking away. But the city had a way of keeping her on the line, like a caller who wouldn't hang up. She couldn't leave it, because leaving meant pretending it might change on its own.

She set the mug down with a soft ding and said the word aloud, her voice unwavering.

"Enough."

The word hung in the quiet, final as a verdict.

By late morning, the clouds had lifted just enough to turn the street to silver. She walked west under the El, coat belted tight, the city carrying its usual scent of rain, oil, and something half-burned.

At 1648 Lake, the grocer nodded from behind the counter. She bought two rolls of film and a packet of batteries—small transactions that said the world was still turning. She lingered by the counter while the clerk cut a duplicate key, the machine whining as brass filings fell onto the mat. Flashlight, duct tape, a lock-pick set hanging on a peg—tools for entry, not defense. She paid cash, folded the receipt into her pocket.

On her way out, she paused by a rack of pocketknives. Chrome handles, slim blades that caught the weak light. She hesitated, then left them where they were. Protection wasn't always a weapon. Sometimes it was preparation.

The apartment dimmed with the weather. Steam curled from the radiator, and somewhere above, the El groaned past like an old thought refusing to die.

She dropped the needle on the phonograph, letting the room fill first with Roberta Flack's *Feel Like Makin' Love*—slow, a voice wrapped in smoke. The record's warmth softened the edges of the day.

Flack followed with Marvin Gaye's *Trouble Man.* Mick used to play that one on terrible nights, said the horns reminded him of headlines—loud, fast, gone too soon. She let the track play out, the static at the end louder than the words. When the record stopped, she didn't lift the arm. She sat in the quiet that followed, city light striping the wall like old film reels.

By dusk, the blinds were half-shut, and the city lights had come alive again—small constellations between storms. She touched the Leica once before leaving, the metal cold beneath her fingers.

"*For the light,*" she whispered, the way Mick used to before every assignment.

She put on her coat, slid the key and the Leica into her pocket, and headed for Ashland.

The walk was short. The purpose wasn't.

Callahan's light would still be burning.

***

28

BARGAIN

Friday, November 21, 1975

The rain had thinned to mist by the time she reached the precinct on Ashland. The city hung between shifts—day half gone; night not yet sure of itself. Fluorescent light spilled through the glass, drained of warmth, telling on itself.

Vivian paused at the side door, the one that always stuck in the frame. She'd been through it before. So had he. The handle gave with a groan, metal on metal—like an old secret opening once more.

The hallway smelled of wax, coffee, and resignation. Her heels found the rhythm of the building's fatigue.

Callahan's office light glowed down the corridor, a square of yellow on the floor. He was where she knew he'd be—jacket off, tie slack, a bottle standing guard beside the cold ashtray.

"Couldn't stay away, huh?" he said, not looking up.

"You still keep late hours," she replied, stepping in. "Figured I'd return the favor."

He finally raised his eyes. The years had crept closer on him—lines deepening, certainty thinning.

She laid her gloves on the desk slowly and deliberately, then placed the small brass key beside them. The tag caught the lamplight.

His jaw tightened. "You don't waste time."

"Neither does the city," she said. "It's chewing through good men while the bad ones hand out paychecks."

He exhaled, leaning back. "You came for the evidence room."

Vivian nodded once. "And for you. You've still got a piece of clean left in you, Tommy. Don't let them use it to bury you."

He gave a short laugh that never reached his eyes. "You think a door and a conscience can fix this place?"

"No," she said. "But opening one and using the other's a start."

She stepped closer, her shadow crossing the desk. "You remember Peter Mitchell? The soldier who came here looking for his sister? You handed him over to me because you knew your precinct wouldn't lift a finger. She's in Potter's Field now, Tommy. Buried under your division's paperwork."

He rubbed a hand over his face. "Don't do that, Viv."

"I will," she snapped. "Because you know what it feels like to lose someone and keep the lie alive, anyway. Every day you sit behind this desk, you add one more ghost to your file."

He stared at her, with nowhere left to hide. Under his breath, almost to himself:

"Every man wants redemption. Trouble is, most wait until the last bell to ask for it."

Vivian's expression softened. "Seamus told me that once. You should've listened when it still cost less."

The silence that followed was thick enough to touch. Rain whispered against the window, patient as guilt.

"You still think you can save this city," he said.

"I think I can make it answer for one lie at a time."

He looked down at the key. The weight seemed to pull his hand toward it before he moved.

"You already have one," he said, nodding at the brass tag. "But it won't get you through the electronic lock. You need me."

"That's why I'm here," she said. "Not for your permission. Your choice."

Callahan's mouth twitched, somewhere between a smirk and a confession. "You always knew how to make a man feel noble while you pushed him off the edge."

Vivian leaned closer, voice soft but steady. "This isn't about nobility. It's about not drowning in the same mud you've been standing in since DeMarco signed that report."

He looked away, then opened the bottom drawer, drew out a second keycard, and set it beside the brass one.

"You didn't get this from me," he said. "If anyone asks, I was at home with a bottle."

She picked up the card, slipping it into her coat. "Hope it's a good one."

He gave a tired half-smile. "You'll make sure of that."

Vivian paused at the door. "Whatever you're holding onto, Tommy—let it go before it buries you. You deserve one clean page."

"Don't tell me I'm the good guy now," he said.

"I'm just saying you don't have to be the bad one."

The rain thickened again outside, drumming faintly on the glass. She turned the knob, then looked back.

"Peter deserved better," she said. "So did Donna. Don't make me add your name to the list."

He nodded once, eyes fixed on the empty spot where the key had been.

Vivian stepped into the hall, her reflection ghosting across the glass panel of his door. Behind her, Callahan poured a single shot, raised it halfway, then set it down untouched.

Down the corridor, the hum of fluorescent light led her toward the stairwell marked **Vice Evidence—Authorized Personnel Only**.

She drew a breath, slid the keycard through the reader, and whispered what passed for a prayer in her line of work.

"*Let the shadows tell the rest.*"

The mechanism clicked—a sound sharp enough to wake the city's ghosts. She went in.

The door sealed behind her, quiet as guilt.

***

29

LEDGER

FRIDAY, NOVEMBER 21, 1975

The lights in the Vice Evidence room buzzed to life one by one, slow as a confession. Rows of steel shelves lined the space, each tagged with numbers that meant nothing to anyone who hadn't written them.

Vivian shut the door behind her and waited a moment, letting the silence settle. The room was colder than the hall—the kind of chill that carried the weight of what people hid. She slipped on her gloves and moved down the first aisle. Folders stacked like bricks. Ledgers bound in fading leather. Cardboard boxes labeled *Property, Confiscated, Vice Division*. Her fingertips trailed across the spines until one label caught her eye—*Wellsford Hotel / March 1974*.

Somewhere beyond the cinderblock wall came the faint crackle of a phone receiver, a pause, then a man's voice—low, deliberate.

"You think I like cleaning up your mess, Callahan?"

The answer was too soft to catch, but the reply wasn't. "Then make it disappear. Or we both go under."

The line went dead. A door closed. Silence folded back into the hum of the lights.

Vivian stayed still until her pulse steadied. Then she moved to the nearest shelf. The binder was heavier than it looked. She set it on the table beneath the flickering light and opened it carefully. The pages smelled of ink and carbon paper—a bureaucrat's perfume.

Receipts. Transfers. Signatures. DeMarco's name—neat, deliberate—appeared over and over like a watermark. But another name surfaced too, printed across an equipment-requisition slip: *Kowalski, L.* The same pawnshop hand who'd stonewalled her on Milwaukee Avenue. The note beside it read *Chain of custody—cleared to Vice / personal hold.*

Vivian's jaw tightened. Lenny hadn't been just another fence; he'd been feeding the division. She turned the page and stopped.

A familiar signature wound across the bottom of the next sheet—Callahan's—but the handwriting wasn't right. The confident loops had thinned into tremors, as if the man holding the pen already knew what it meant to betray himself. She traced the ink with her gloved finger.

"You knew," she murmured. From her purse, she drew the Leica, loaded with fresh film. Frame, focus, flash, advance. The rhythm steadied her pulse—Mick's rhythm. He'd once said the camera caught what courage couldn't.

She shot the relevant pages—DeMarco's authorizations, Kowalski's supply slips, Callahan's faltering name. One after another, each exposure caught a little more of the rot.

Halfway through the roll, she noticed a drawer at the far end of the table, half open, a file jutting out like a tongue. She pulled it free. Inside were three photographs—girls lined up for booking, one of them unmistakable. Donna Mitchell. On the back, typed in red ink: *Evidence transferred / D.M.—DeMarco.*

Vivian's stomach went cold. Proof—at last.

The overhead bulb flickered twice, the hum deepening into a pulse. She froze. A faint sound drifted from the far end of the aisle—the click of a latch, the whisper of perfume cutting through dust. Sweet, sharp, expensive. Not department issue.

She turned, listening. The air carried a trace of cigarette smoke and something else—vinyl, rain, motion. For a heartbeat, she thought she saw a silhouette near the door—the line of a narrow shoulder, the gleam of dark hair. Then it was gone.

She waited, breath shallow, until the silence closed again. Then she finished the roll, slid the binder back into place, and wiped a smear of dust from the table. The evidence room hummed on, pretending to be empty.

In the corridor, a narrow strip of light spilled from Callahan's office. He sat behind his desk, the same bottle untouched beside the glass.

Vivian stepped through the doorway and laid the brass key on the blotter. "You did right," she said.

He looked up slowly. "Did I?"

"I know how this looks," Callahan said. He hesitated, then shook his head. "No—I know what it is." He didn't say anything after that.

She nodded once. "You'll know on Monday."

Her coat brushed the frame as she turned away, footsteps fading down the hall.

Callahan sat motionless, eyes fixed on the key. He reached for it, then stopped halfway, fingers hovering above the metal. The tremor in his hand matched the one in his signature.

He thought of what she'd said about Peter, about truth, about ghosts that never left a man alone. Once, he'd had a chance with her—back when he still believed the job meant justice and that courage didn't always end in paperwork. He'd lost both the day he turned away from the truth.

The hum of the fluorescent light deepened, carrying the sound of her footsteps until they disappeared. Callahan poured the drink at last, but the whiskey just sat there, reflecting the door she'd walked through. He didn't drink it.

Outside, the rain had slowed to a whisper, and somewhere beyond the glass, the city kept breathing. Vivian still had Mick's Leica in her hand—the same lens that once captured wars half a world away. Now it held another kind of battlefield: closer, quieter, no less brutal.

Monday was coming, and with it, the truth they'd both helped unlock.

***

30

REPORTER

SATURDAY, NOVEMBER 22, 1975

The Tribune building was half-asleep when Vivian arrived just after dawn, Saturday. The city was quiet in that rarest of hours—too early for the morning crowd, too late for the drunks to care.

Inside, the newsroom hummed faintly—presses groaning in the basement, a radio whispering near the city desk. The overhead lights buzzed but hadn't yet warmed to life.

Cynthia Vega sat alone at the far end of the room, hair pulled into a loose knot, sleeves rolled, a paper cup of coffee steaming beside a half-eaten sweet roll. A stack of notes and carbon sheets sat at her elbow, her typewriter waiting mid-line. She looked up when Vivian stepped in.

"Vivian Kessler," she said, a smile breaking through the fatigue. "I haven't seen you since—hell—since Mags left office. She talked about you all the time."

Vivian managed a faint nod. "Mags talked about you, too. Said you were one of the last reporters who remembered what truth costs."

Vega chuckled softly, brushing crumbs from her notebook. "That sounds like her. So, what dragged you here before sunrise?"

Vivian didn't answer right away. She looked every inch the professional—brown coat belted tight, gloves in hand—but the eyes behind it hadn't slept in two days.

She set her purse on the desk. "A friend in the Tribune darkroom owed Mick a favor," she whispered. "They ran these for me overnight."

Then she slid a thick manila envelope across the blotter. "Everything you'll need for Monday's front page."

Vega arched a brow, loosening the string. Inside were contact sheets, typed pages, and three black-and-white photographs. She spread them across the desk, light catching the glossy paper.

The first showed ledgers stamped *Vice Division—Confidential.*

The second, a requisition slip bearing Kowalski, L.

The third—Callahan's unsteady signature above DeMarco's bold one.

"Jesus," Vega murmured. "This is the Wellsford. I knew it wasn't just a rumor."

Vivian's tone stayed low. "You'll find Donna Mitchell in there, too. File marked D.M., transferred by DeMarco. No mistake."

Vega's jaw tightened. "You got these yourself?"

Vivian nodded. "The room was supposed to be empty. It wasn't."

"Meaning?"

"Someone else was there. Perfume, cigarette smoke. Maybe one girl still breathing. Maybe not."

Vega studied the overlapping names. "DeMarco's mark is everywhere in this. Funny thing—he's been sliding out of favor for months. Word at City Hall says he backed the wrong alderman. Mob boys stopped covering his mess. He's either getting cut loose or looking for a way out."

Vivian watched her, unreadable. "Maybe he saw what they were doing to the girls and couldn't stomach it anymore."

Vega shrugged, chewing her pencil. "Or maybe he tried to trade his conscience for protection. Hard to tell in this town which side's cleaner."

She set the photo down, gaze steady. "Either way, you've given me the rope. Let's see who hangs on."

Vivian said nothing. The weariness in her eyes wasn't victory—it was the kind that comes after truth, when there's nothing left to chase but consequences.

Vega flipped through the contact sheets, tracing the frames on the sheet with her fingertip. "These shots—they're Mick's Leica, aren't they? I'd know that style anywhere. He used to bring me prints when I was still on copy duty."

Vivian's voice softened. "He left it to me. Figured it should keep working."

Vega nodded slowly, scanning the evidence again. "These signatures alone could burn half of Vice. You've got DeMarco, Kowalski, and the bridge right into Callahan's division. If the editors have any guts left, this runs front page Monday morning."

"That's the plan."

Vega took a sip of coffee, then set it beside the photographs. "You understand what this means, right? If this prints, some of those names won't just lose their badges—they'll try to bury the story and anyone tied to it."

Vivian met her eyes. "They already buried the girls. You just need to make them answer for it."

For a long moment, the only sound was the presses thundering below—the deep metallic heartbeat of the building. Vega tapped her pencil once against the desk. "Mags used to say the truth only matters if it stains."

"She was right."

Vega gave a small, tired smile. "She'd like that you're still out there making a mess of things for the right reasons."

Vivian turned toward the door. "You'll have everything you need by Monday. Make it count."

"I will," Vega said. "And Viv—"

Vivian paused.

"Try to get some sleep. You look like you've been up since Watergate."

Vivian's mouth curved into the faintest shadow of a smile. "Close enough."

Vega watched her go, the brown coat vanishing into the half-light. The door closed with a hush that carried the smell of rain and ink.

She looked down at the photos again, the names, the faces, the grain of truth trapped in silver. Then she whispered what Mags would've said, half prayer, half promise.

"Let it stain."

***

31

— • —

Fallout

Monday, November 24, 1975

By eight o'clock Monday morning, November 24, the city had already read her work without knowing her name.

The Tribune headline stretched across the front page like a wound:

VICE DIVISION UNDER FIRE—INTERNAL FILES REVEAL SYSTEMIC CORRUPTION.

Outside, the streets glistened from the night's rain. The air felt lighter, as if Chicago had finally exhaled. Trains roared above Lake Street, shaking loose drops from the girders.

Vivian walked toward The Brass Rail with the paper folded under her arm. She hadn't slept since Friday, but she moved with the same calm precision that always marked the end of a job—the part where everything looked away and she accepted what remained.

Inside, the bar was dim, the jukebox dark. Eddie stood behind the counter, hands moving out of habit, a cup turning slow between them. Steam curled from the coffee urn beside him.

Frank sat two stools down, reading the Tribune with his glasses halfway down his nose. Seamus was in his usual place by the jukebox, cigarette burning slow.

Vivian took her seat in the center of the bar. Eddie poured from the pot before she could ask.

"Morning, Viv."

"Morning."

She wrapped her hands around the cup, grateful for the heat more than the taste.

Frank folded the paper and set it in front of her. "Hell of a way to start the week."

Vivian looked down at the headline, then at him. "Looks like Vega came through."

"She did," Frank said, with a faint smile creasing his face. "Mags would've been proud. So am I."

Vivian nodded once, eyes lowering to the coffee. "It's her story now."

The words hung there, quiet as steam off her cup.

Eddie set down his rag, voice low. "Word on the street is De-Marco's gone underground. Some say Internal Affairs is hunting him. Others say he took a payoff and vanished downstate."

Vivian didn't flinch. "He'll surface. Men like that always do."

Seamus took a long drag from his cigarette and exhaled slowly. "This place settles its accounts in its own time."

Vivian lifted her coffee, the steam fogging her glasses for a moment before clearing. "Some debts keep collecting interest."

Silence stretched through the Rail, thick but not uncomfortable. The trains above clattered on, indifferent.

Frank leaned forward, elbows on the bar. "You did what the rest of us stopped trying to do, Viv. You made the truth stick."

She shook her head lightly. "It's just ink, Frank. Tomorrow there'll be another story."

"Maybe," he said. "But today, this one's yours."

Vivian looked at him then—the old detective's steady pride, the quiet respect he rarely showed anyone. For the first time in days, her shoulders eased.

The door at the far end opened, letting in a blade of light and the faint scent of rain. Loretta slipped inside, coat cinched tight, eyes scanning the room until they landed on Vivian.

"Heard your name in the paper, sugar," she said, voice low but warm. "Didn't need to read it to know it was you."

Vivian gave her a faint smile. "City had to listen to someone."

Loretta nodded. "'Bout time it was a woman." She tipped her chin toward the headline, then moved down the bar, ordering coffee instead of whiskey.

The door shut behind her, and the quiet folded back in.

Vivian traced a finger along the newspaper's edge. The photo of the Tribune Building filled half the page, framed by the headline. For a moment, she pictured Peter—holding the same edition in some kitchen far from here, showing it to his parents, maybe saying her name aloud just once. There'd be no comfort in it, but there'd be truth. And that would have to do.

Eddie refilled her cup without asking. "No charge."

"Thanks, Eddie."

He gave a small nod. "City's buying this one."

The jukebox clicked on by itself, as if the room needed sound again. Dinah Washington's voice slipped through the speakers—soft, tired, and certain. *This Bitter Earth*.

Vivian didn't look back.

Seamus smiled through his beard. "Seems the lady's got perfect timing."

Vivian didn't reply. She just watched the coffee swirl in her cup, the reflection of the jukebox light trembling on its surface.

Outside, the morning sun pushed through the thinning clouds, spilling gold across the wet street.

For a moment, The Rail felt like the still point of the city—truth printed, debts named, ghosts stirring.

She rose from her stool and stepped into the morning, the city waiting to be ordinary again.

***

32

— · —

Last Walk

Monday, November 24, 1975

By nine o'clock, the trains above Lake Street were already running full, their rhythm steady now, ordinary again. Morning had shaken off the rain and gone back to pretending nothing had happened.

Vivian walked with her collar turned up against the damp wind, the folded Tribune still under her arm. Each headline she passed on the corner rack was already soft around the edges—yesterday's fire cooling into print.

A delivery truck backfired near Union Park, scattering a small flock of pigeons into the gray morning air. The street smelled of wet concrete, coffee, and the faint sweetness of bakery rolls from the corner deli. A group of children waited near the curb for the school bus, backpacks at their feet, playing a quick game of tag to keep warm. Their laughter carried through the chill—clear and bright against the steel and brick.

Vivian slowed, smiling despite herself. Life always found its way back to the surface.

From an open apartment window, a familiar voice drifted down—a WGN announcer easing into the day.

"Sunny skies ahead for Chicago this afternoon... temperatures climbing into the fifties by evening... the Hawks take on New York tonight at the Stadium... "

The words carried on the breeze, ordinary and whole—the news she could finally bear to hear.

At the corner of Lake and Ashland, she stopped to look east. The clouds were thinning, the skyline sharp again against the morning light. The Sears Tower rose first, black steel clean and absolute; beside it, the Hancock caught the sun along its cross-braced ribs. Between them, smaller now but still proud, the Prudential Building gleamed like a memory of what the city once believed was enough.

She remembered being a girl, holding her mother's hand downtown, watching that first tower reach above everything else. Then, years later, seeing the Hancock climb higher, modern and unstoppable. Now the Sears eclipsed them both—a monument to how Chicago never stopped building over its ghosts.

The towers told the whole story: what the city destroyed, it also dreamed.

She crossed Ashland. Hal was out front in his robe again, a Bears sweatshirt showing beneath it, the same chipped mug in hand.

"Morning, Miss Viv!" he called, grinning wide. "You're looking more like yourself today."

She gave him a tired but genuine smile. "Guess the city finally blinked first." He laughed softly. "Ain't it always?"

Vivian climbed the steps, each one echoing the El's steady rumble overhead. On the landing she paused, looking back down the block—the puddles, the sunlight, the kids' bright jackets near the stop, their laughter fading as the bus approached.

Inside, the hallway smelled of steam and dust, familiar and warm. She unlocked her door and stepped into the quiet.

The apartment looked the same—same table, same blinds, same coffee cup waiting beside the radio. She set the newspaper down, hung her coat, and crossed to the living-room window, where the three towers stood clear against the pale blue morning.

She watched them for a long moment, then reached for the phonograph.

From the shelf, she drew a record sleeve. On the corner, in Mick's handwriting, it read: *For the road ahead.*

She smiled faintly and set it on the turntable.

When the first bars of Ringo Starr's *Photograph* played, the room filled with a quiet ache—nostalgia and longing wrapped in melody. The song spoke of faces remembered, places left behind, love caught forever in a single frame.

The record spun slowly, the green apple on the label blurring into a pale circle. Vivian stood by the window as the music played, her reflection faint against the glow.

She moved to her chair—the blinds cutting the morning light into long, trembling bands across her face. As the needle drifted toward the record's center, the music softened to a whisper.

Outside, a train roared past, scattering sparks into the air like falling stars. The reflection in the windowpane shimmered—three towers rising steadily in the glass as the last notes faded.

The turntable clicked. The arm lifted, returning to its rest.

Vivian exhaled. The city moved with her.

For once, it didn't feel like a warning. It felt like grace.

***

— · —

THE SOUNDTRACK OF THE MISSING
FLOWER CHILD

The following songs appear throughout the story, listed by part and in the order in which they are heard. Titles and artist credits reflect their cultural presence within the story's 1975 setting.

Part I—November Rain

- *RHINESTONE COWBOY*, GLEN CAMPBELL (1975), CAPITOL RECORDS—SAFE HAVEN

- *HAVE YOU SEEN HER*, THE CHI-LITES (1971), BRUNSWICK RECORDS—THE RAIL

- *AIN'T NO SUNSHINE*, BILL WITHERS (1971), SUSSEX RECORDS—LETTERS

- *MIDNIGHT TRAIN TO GEORGIA*, GLADYS KNIGHT & THE PIPS (1973), BUDDAH RECORDS—LETTERS (CLOSING BEAT)

Part II—The Dark City

- *I KNOW A PLACE*, PETULA CLARK (1965), PYE

RECORDS—MICK

- *KILLING ME SOFTLY WITH HIS SONG*, ROBERTA FLACK (1973), ATLANTIC RECORDS—CALLAHAN

- *TURN BACK THE HANDS OF TIME*, TYRONE DAVIS (1970), DAKAR RECORDS—RONNIE

- *BORN TO RUN*, BRUCE SPRINGSTEEN (1975), COLUMBIA RECORDS—RONNIE (SECOND BEAT)

- *FOR THE LOVE OF MONEY*, THE O'JAYS (1973), PHILADELPHIA INTERNATIONAL RECORDS—VORTEX (ENTRANCE)

- *I'M NOT IN LOVE*, 10CC (1975), MERCURY RECORDS—VORTEX (INTERIOR)

- *FAME*, DAVID BOWIE (1975), RCA RECORDS—VORTEX (EXIT)

- *LOVE TO LOVE YOU BABY*, DONNA SUMMER (1975), OASIS/CASABLANCA—NIKKI

- *LYIN' EYES*, EAGLES (1975), ASYLUM RECORDS—RECORDS

Part III—Glass and Fire

- *LANDSLIDE*, FLEETWOOD MAC (1975), REPRISE RECORDS—POTTER'S FIELD (CAB RADIO)

- *DREAM ON*, AEROSMITH (1973), COLUMBIA RECORDS—POTTER'S FIELD (DISTANT HIGHWAY RADIO)

- *FOR THE GOOD TIMES*, AL GREEN (1972), HI RECORDS—MADAM

- *YOU'RE THE FIRST, THE LAST, MY EVERYTHING*, BARRY WHITE (1974), 20TH CENTURY RECORDS—TRAP

- *THIS BITTER EARTH*, DINAH WASHINGTON (1960), MERCURY RECORDS—AFTERMATH

Part IV—The Long Morning

- *FEEL LIKE MAKIN LOVE*, ROBERTA FLACK (1974), ATLANTIC RECORDS—CHOICE (PHONOGRAPH)

- *TROUBLE MAN*, MARVIN GAYE (1972), TAMLA RECORDS—CHOICE (CONTINUED)

- *THIS BITTER EARTH*, DINAH WASHINGTON (1960), MERCURY RECORDS—FALLOUT (JUKEBOX REPRISE)

- *PHOTOGRAPH*, RINGO STARR (1973), APPLE RECORDS—LAST WALK

***

— · —

Acknowledgments

This book exists because of the generosity of a small circle of readers and supporters who offered insight, patience, and encouragement along the way. Their thoughtful feedback strengthened the work, and their belief in the story made finishing it possible. I'm deeply grateful.

***

ABOUT THE AUTHOR

B.A. Montes writes character-driven noir set against the social and political fault lines of 1960s and 1970s Chicago. Drawing on a lifelong engagement with technology, education, and the quiet complexities of everyday life, his work explores power, loyalty, and the choices people make when certainty is no longer available. *The Missing Flower Child* is the first novella in the **Kessler Files**.

***

THE KESSLER FILES

STORIES OF CHICAGO, 1948-1978

These stories trace Vivian Kessler's path through a changing Chicago. Each case stands alone, but together they reveal the forces—quiet and visible—that shape her life.

The Missing Flower Child

A Vivian Kessler Case—November 1975

Vivian is pulled into a missing-person investigation on Chicago's North Side—one that exposes the quiet machinery of influence, loyalty, and control shaping the city's hidden life.

Additional stories in **The Kessler Files** are forthcoming.

***